ENERGY EFT
For TEENAGERS

The Simple Solution
For Success & Happiness

Paula Kennedy

Energy EFT For Teenagers
The Simple Solution for Success & Happiness

Print: ISBN 978-1-908269-65-2
Digital: ISBN 978-1-908269-66-9
First Edition

Published by
DragonRising Publishing
The Guild of Energists Ltd.
PO Box 3175
Eastbourne
BN21 9PG
United Kingdom
www.DragonRising.com

ENERGY EFT
For TEENAGERS

The Simple Solution
For Success & Happiness

Paula Kennedy

REVIEW

Wendy Birse is a highly experienced and qualified GOE Energist and Trainer. She sent us this review of Energy EFT for Teenagers: The Simple Solution for Success and Happiness. We are pleased to share her comments with you.

> *I was delighted to discover this book which presents EFT in a practical and straightforward way for young people. It specifically addresses many of the issues that teenagers in particular face while making it clear that EFT is a tool they can adapt to suit themselves in any situation. Paula Kennedy has done a great job in making EFT accessible and acceptable to some of the people who may need it most!*
>
> Wendy Birse, mother and grandmother

DISCLAIMER

The contents of this self-help book are purely for educational purposes. This information should not be used to replace medical help, advice, or be a substitute treatment for any medical or psychological condition. Always consult your doctor or other medical health professional if in any doubt.

This self-help guide is a gentle introduction to the world of Energy EFT (Emotional Freedom Technique). It is written in a format that is simple for adults, teachers and teenagers to understand and access. It is also a good reference for parents, teachers and care workers. It is advisable for a parent, care worker or teacher to read through the book with a teenager under the age of 18. Parents, teachers and care workers may also greatly benefit from using the contents of this book to relieve their daily stresses. Group tapping sessions can be very beneficial for all members of the family or in the classroom.

Although the results and clinical trials of using Energy EFT have been very encouraging and positive, it is still in its early years of development. Therefore, anyone using this book is totally responsible for their own well-being.

MY MISSION

I am on a mission to spread knowledge about and the use of Energy EFT. I hope my book will help to introduce Energy EFT to families and I would love to see it used in schools to help children and teenagers with nearly all the problems they must face while growing up. Please read it, use it, share it, talk about it and, hopefully, greatly benefit from it.

THANKS

To Nick Klynsmith for the wonderful graphics.

To my three wonderful daughters, Sophie, Daisy and Millie Kennedy for teaching me that being a Mum has many challenges but also many amazing moments and treasured memories. Also for being the inspiration to put Energy EFT into a book that will help other teenagers with any problems they may encounter while growing up.

To my beautiful Mum, Erin Fryer, who has stood by, supported and trialled all my therapies and helped me when I dealt with the challenges of having children on the Autistic Spectrum. Also for being there for me through thick and thin.

To my kind, loving partner, Julian Gammon, for helping me through all of what life has thrown at us and still being there on the other side.

Also, many thanks to Gary Craig and Silvia Hartmann, because without them I would never have started this journey.

CONTENTS

INTRODUCTION TO ENERGY EFT

Life isn't always easy. We all have our ups and downs but sometimes there are situations that affect us much more than we would like or over which we have little control.

These could be caused by a falling out with a friend or feeling like we don't fit in, or we may have daily struggles with family or school life.

Sometimes things that happen in our lives can cause our emotions to work in overdrive. We can become overly sensitive to things that don't usually bother us but that in a particular instance can cause us to become angry, overwhelmed, stressed, scared, depressed, anxious, sad, or just to feel let down and like the world is against us.

Does any of this sound familiar to you? If so, help is at hand in the form of Energy EFT (Emotional Freedom Technique), also known as tapping.

Energy EFT is a simple form of acupuncture/acupressure, but without the needles. You add in a few relevant words, a bit of psychology and gently tap away all the emotions that are depleting or clogging up your energy body.

Sometimes you may yawn while you tap. This is perfectly normal. It is just your body releasing negative thoughts and emotions.

By releasing all of these stresses and anxieties in your body and mind you should start to feel much better and your daily life can begin to improve as a result.

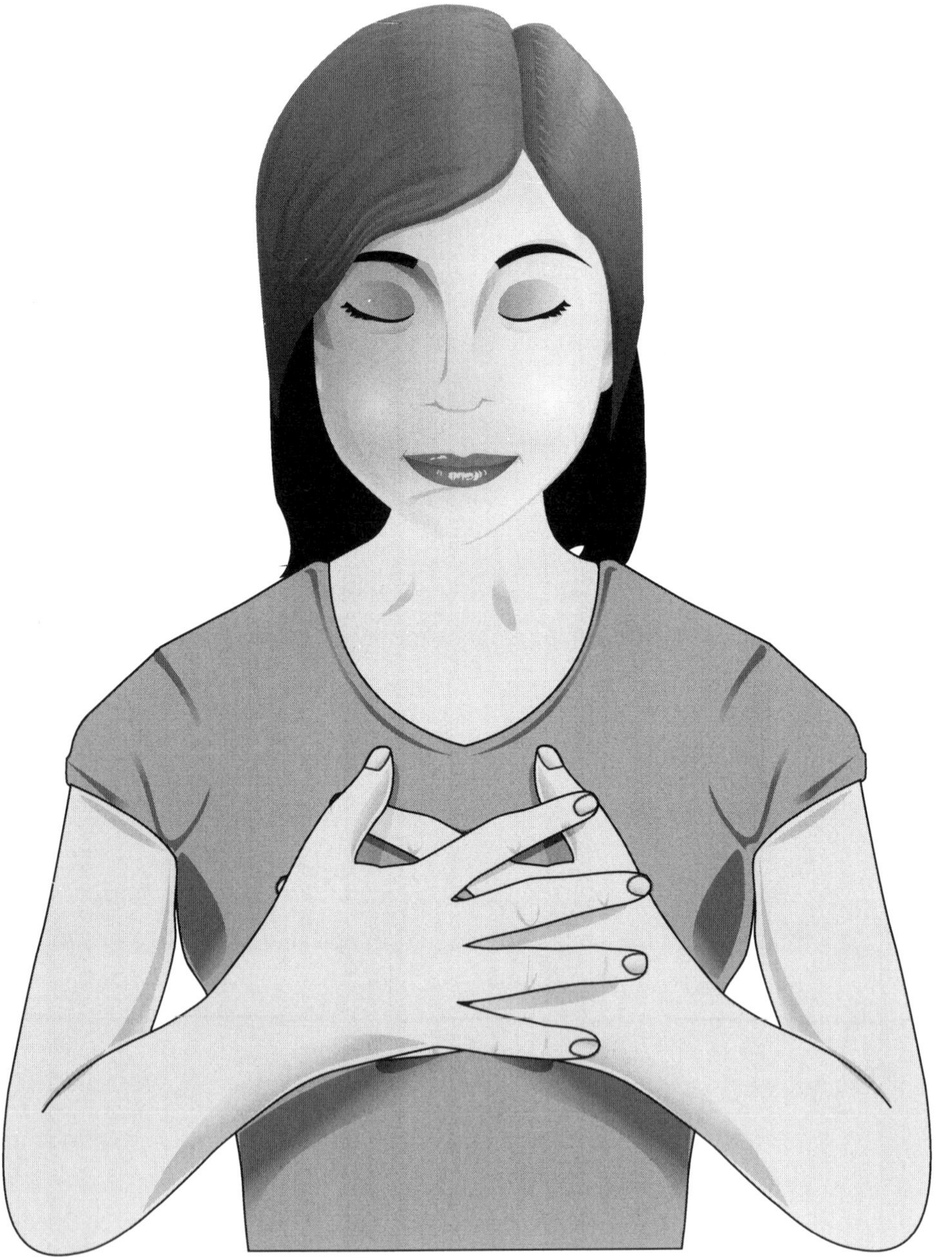

Figure 1 The Heart Healing Position

Tapping is a medication-free, painless therapy that can be done *anywhere*, even discreetly under the table on your thumb and finger points where no-one can see what you're doing. You can tap, hold or even massage the tapping points, whichever way you prefer. There is no right or wrong way to tap, so you can experiment with whichever way you find is the easiest and most comfortable for you.

Tapping can help on some level with almost anything that affects your emotional or physical well-being: depression, stress, anxiety, anger, eating disorders, self-harming, bullying, grief/ trauma, low self-esteem, peer pressure, exam nerves, ADHD, hormones, concentration, sports performance, moodiness, confidence issues or just simply feeling fed up and emotional.

THE HEART HEALING POSITION

At the beginning and end of every round of tapping, the hands should be placed on your heart in what is known as the Heart Healing position (see Figure 1) and take three long breaths. Take your time and make sure the breaths are good and deep. The Heart Healing position and the breaths are a very important part of the process, and allow you to really tune in to how you are feeling.

The Heart Healing position can also be used as an emergency tool when you feel everything is getting to be too much and you don't have the time or space to tap, or you are in a situation where tapping is not possible. Simply adopt the Heart Healing position, take three long, deep breaths, and tell yourself that you are OK and you can deal with the situation.

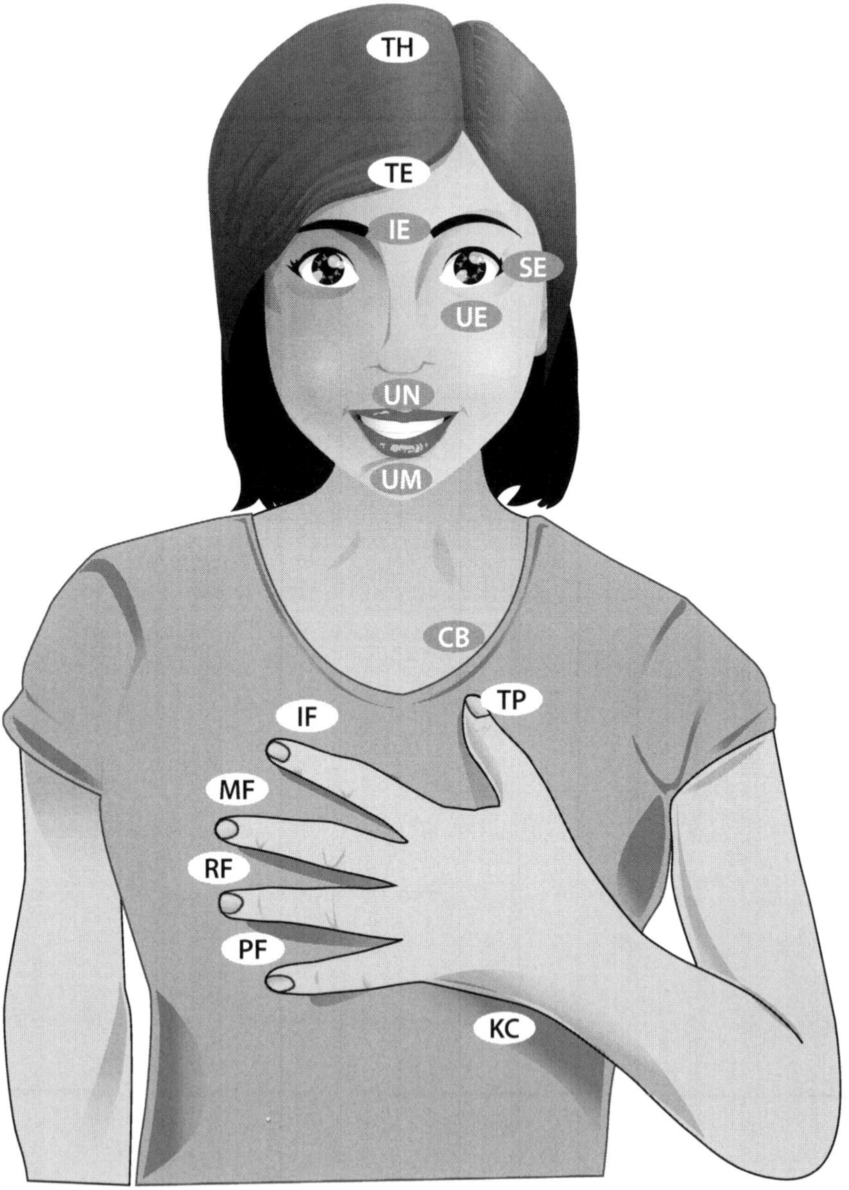

Figure 2 The Tapping Points

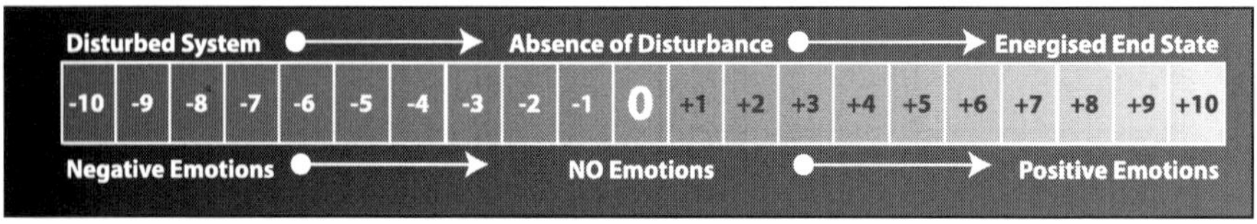

Figure 3 The Tapping Scale

INTRODUCTION TO THE TAPPING POINTS

There are 14 tapping points (see Figure 2). They are: (1) the top of the head point, or TH; (2) the third eye point, or TE; (3) the inner eyebrow point, or IE; (4) the side of the eye point, or SE; (5) the under the eye point, or UE; (6) the under the nose point, or UN; (7) the under the mouth point, or UM; (8) the collar bone point, or CB; (9) the thumb point, or TP; (10) the index finger point, or IF; (11) the middle finger point, or MF; (12) the ring finger point, or RF; (13) the pinky finger point, or PF; and (14) the karate chop point, or KC.

Tapping on body points is done directly on the point. Tapping on the finger points is usually done to the side of the nail bed on the fleshy part of the skin. Tapping on the karate chop point can be done either with a finger or by tapping the point gently against the thumb edge of the other hand.

You can tap to relieve negative feelings or tap to increase positive feelings. Tapping for either kind of feeling follows the same pattern. First, determine what kind of emotion you are dealing with and rate that emotion using the Tapping Scale (see Figure 3); second, give the tapping session a title; third, whether you are tapping on a negative emotion or a positive emotion, begin and end each tapping session with your hands in the Heart Healing position and take three deep breaths in and out; and fourth, during tapping say a series of statements for each point. The only difference between tapping to relieve a negative feeling and tapping to increase a positive feeling is the title you give to the tapping session and the statements you use while tapping.

Let's start with an example of tapping to relieve a negative feeling.

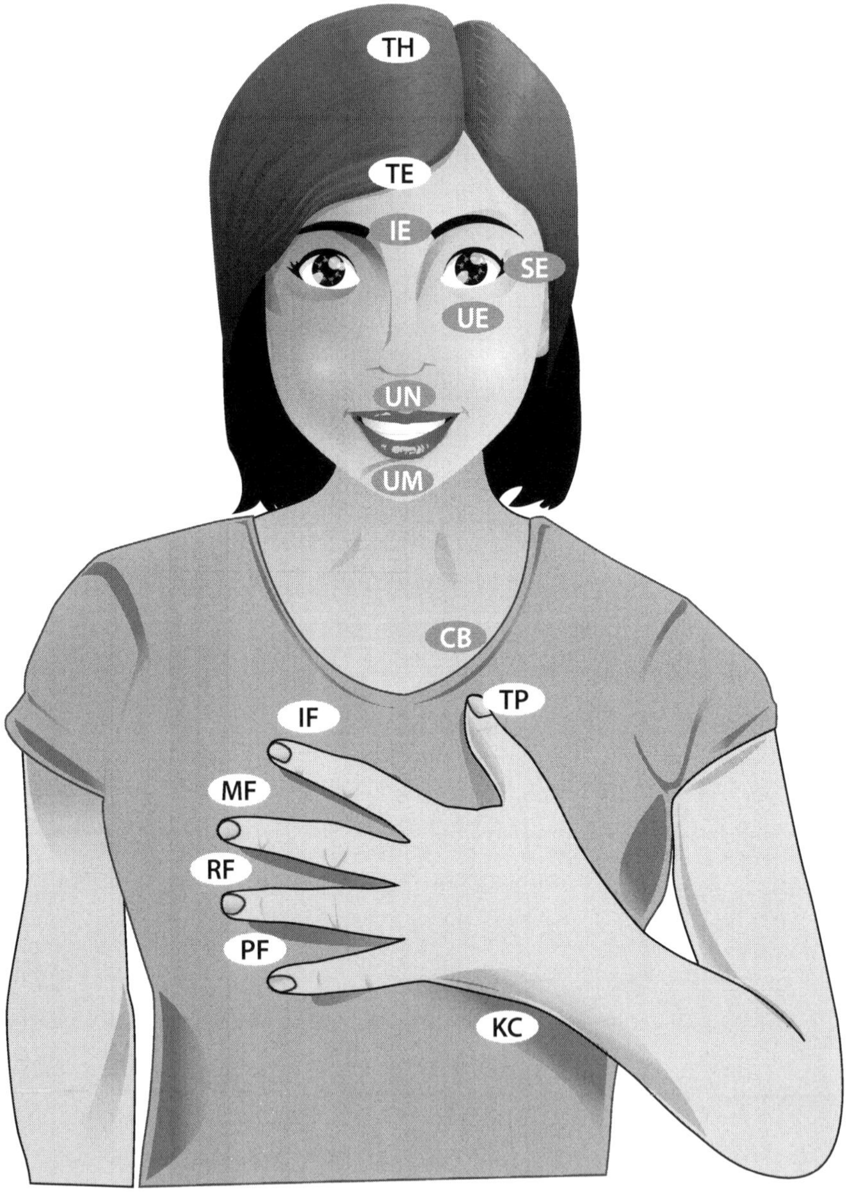
TH
TE
IE
SE
UE
UN
UM
CB
TP
IF
MF
RF
PF
KC

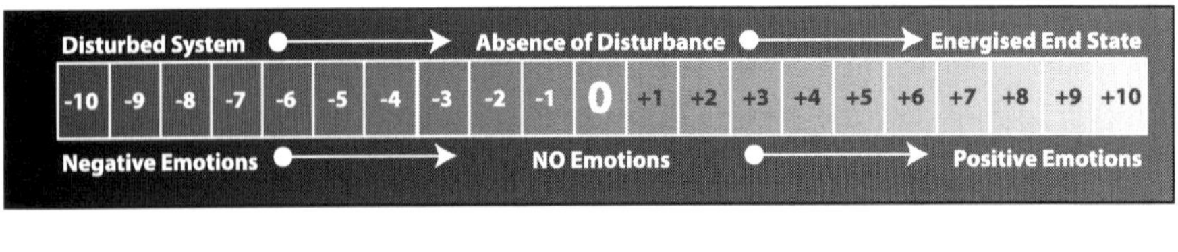
Disturbed System
Absence of Disturbance
Energised End State
-10 -9 -8 -7 -6 -5 -4 -3 -2 -1 0 +1 +2 +3 +4 +5 +6 +7 +8 +9 +10
Negative Emotions
NO Emotions
Positive Emotions

Tapping on a Negative Feeling

While tapping on a negative feeling, tune into the emotions you want to release. For this example, let's use being anxious about speaking in front of the class.

Start by choosing a number on the Tapping Scale. The Scale measures how you are feeling, from a –10 to a +10. The Scale is used as a guide to help you measure the intensity of your stress, anxiety, pain, etc., and the number for any given situation will be different for each person. The worst feeling ever would be a –10. At zero you would feel neutral. The most amazing you could ever feel would be a +10.

If you have a problem or feel stressed you will usually feel pretty negative and this will give you a minus reading on the Tapping Scale. When looking at the Scale, a number will usually come to you and hopefully, with a few rounds of tapping, you can improve this number and move it into the plus numbers on the Scale. This will help you know the tapping is helping.

Say you chose a –5 for how bad this problem makes you feel at that moment. Remember that number while you start your first round of tapping so you can compare it to the number you will choose at the end of the tapping round.

Tune into how you are feeling. Notice where in your body this problem seems to affect you: do you get a constricted feeling in your throat and clam up, feel flushed, feel a little sick to your stomach, or maybe get a tightening sensation in your chest? Whatever feelings this problem fires up, remember what they are so you can use them for later comparison.

Now give your problem or stress a title, such as, 'I Don't Like Talking in Front of the Class'. Place your hands over your

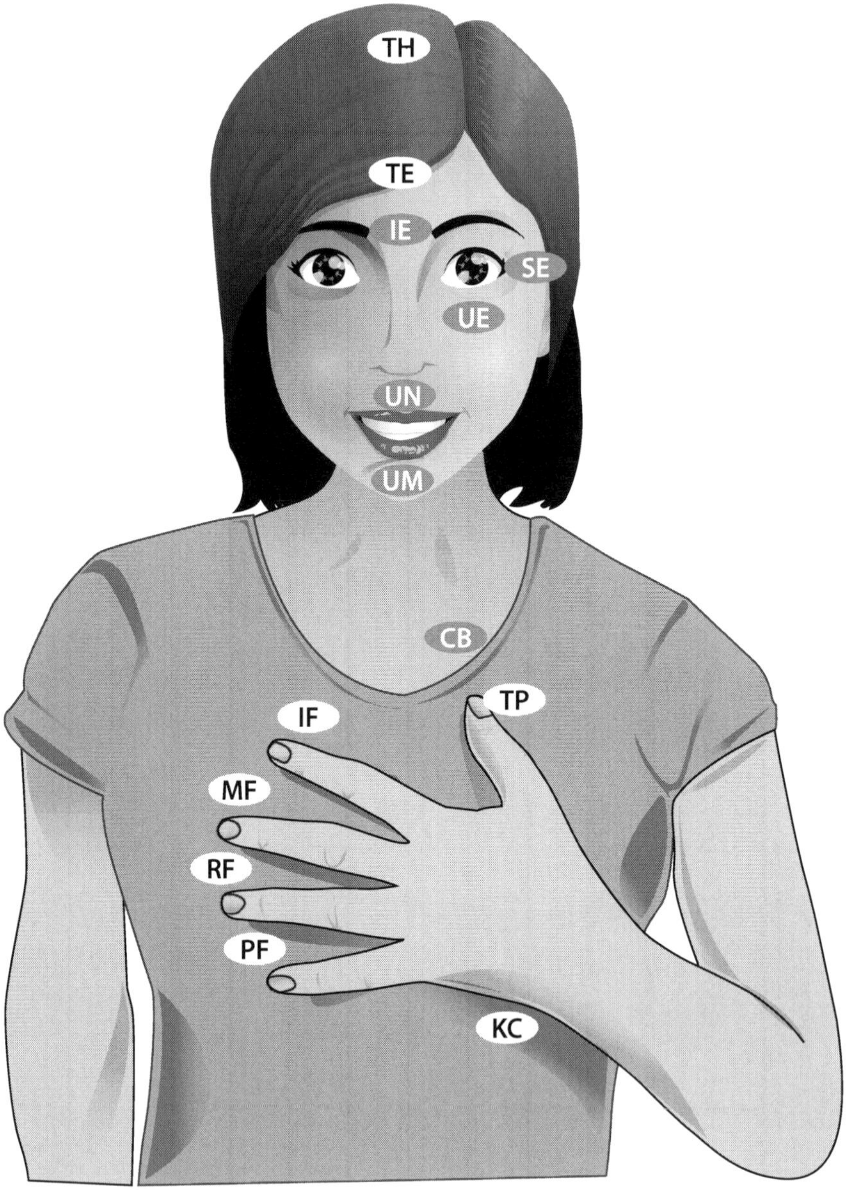

Disturbed System →										Absence of Disturbance →										Energised End State
-10	-9	-8	-7	-6	-5	-4	-3	-2	-1	0	+1	+2	+3	+4	+5	+6	+7	+8	+9	+10
Negative Emotions →										NO Emotions →										Positive Emotions

heart in the Heart Healing position, take three deep breaths and state your title.

Using your index finger, usually of your dominant hand, tap gently about 6 or 7 times on each of the points starting with the TH point, working your way down through the TE, IE, SE, UE, UN and UM points, and ending the body points at the CB point. Then you move to the hand points, starting at the TP point, tapping each finger sequentially, and ending on the KC point. While you are tapping, say the following statements associated with each point. The statements provided are only examples. If any of the statement sequences in this book don't feel right, make up your own that do. Just remember to tap on negative feelings first, focusing on improving those feelings, before moving on to a more positive tapping session.

Sample Tapping Statements

TH = All this fear.

TE = I am really scared.

IE = Worried everyone will laugh at me.

SE = I might mess up my words.

UE = Scared to speak in front of everyone.

UN = I am so scared.

UM = Holding all this fear.

CB = All this fear in my body.

TP = I choose to feel in control.

IF = I choose to let it go.

MF = All this fear.

RF = In every cell of my body.

PF = I choose to release it now.

KC = I choose to feel calm and confident.

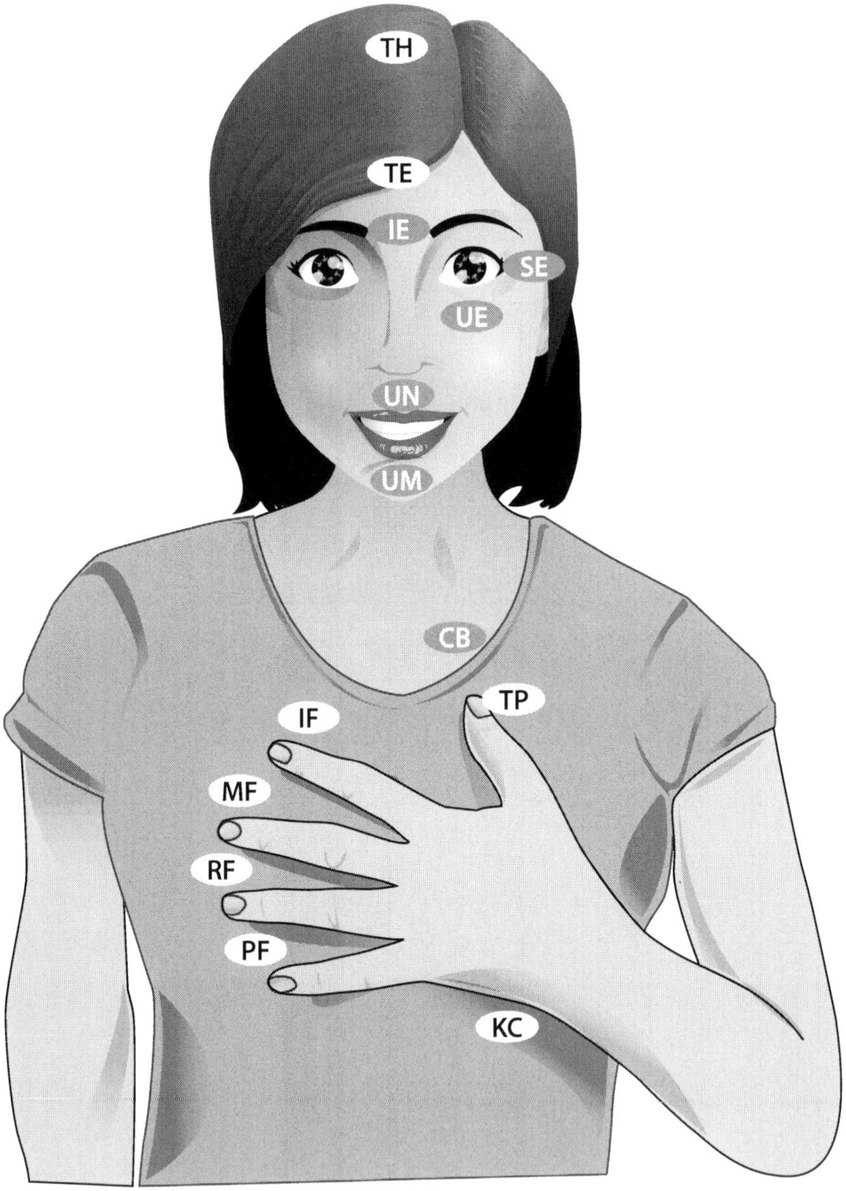
TH
TE
IE
SE
UE
UN
UM
CB
TP
IF
MF
RF
PF
KC

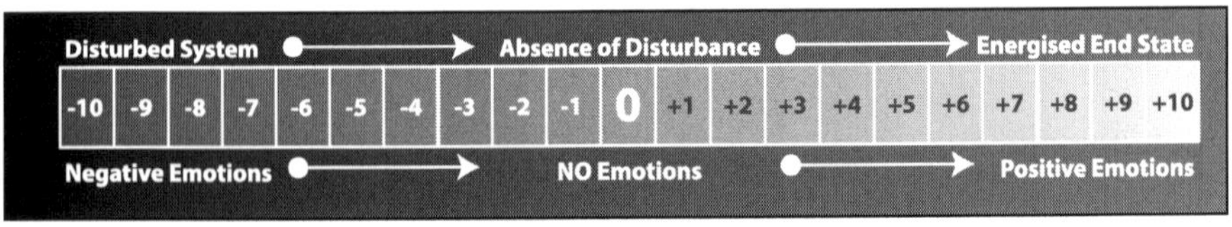
Disturbed System
Absence of Disturbance
Energised End State
-10 -9 -8 -7 -6 -5 -4 -3 -2 -1 0 +1 +2 +3 +4 +5 +6 +7 +8 +9 +10
Negative Emotions
NO Emotions
Positive Emotions

Use whatever words best describe your fear or your humiliation or your anxiety. You can tap on each point and just say, 'this fear' or 'this stress', or any other feelings that have come up, or you could be more specific by saying things such as, 'This fear I am feeling in my stomach' or 'This fear I am feeling in my chest'. Being specific will help you get to the root of the problem.

After your first round of tapping, place your hands over your heart in the Heart Healing position and take three deep breaths to let go of all the negative stress, anxiety or fear. Tune in to how you are feeling and look at the Tapping Scale again.

Choose a number that relates to how you are feeling now. Maybe it has changed to a –3. Have the feelings of worry, fear or stress that you noticed earlier in your body lessened? Do you feel better already? Tap another round or two until you feel really relaxed and are no longer worried about talking in front of the class.

Choose a number that relates to where are you now on the Scale. Perhaps it has gone to a –1 or even a neutral zero, and it no longer affects you at all. If you aren't yet at zero, keep tapping a few more rounds until you are at a zero or a +1, maybe even higher, and are starting to feel even better. Now it's time to tap for a more positive emotion.

Tapping on a Happy Feeling

Once you are done tapping on a negative feeling and have improved your location on the Tapping Scale, do a happy, positive round of tapping to make you feel even better. You could choose any of the positive words from the list in the next paragraph. You can also add in some of your own to make up your own tapping script!

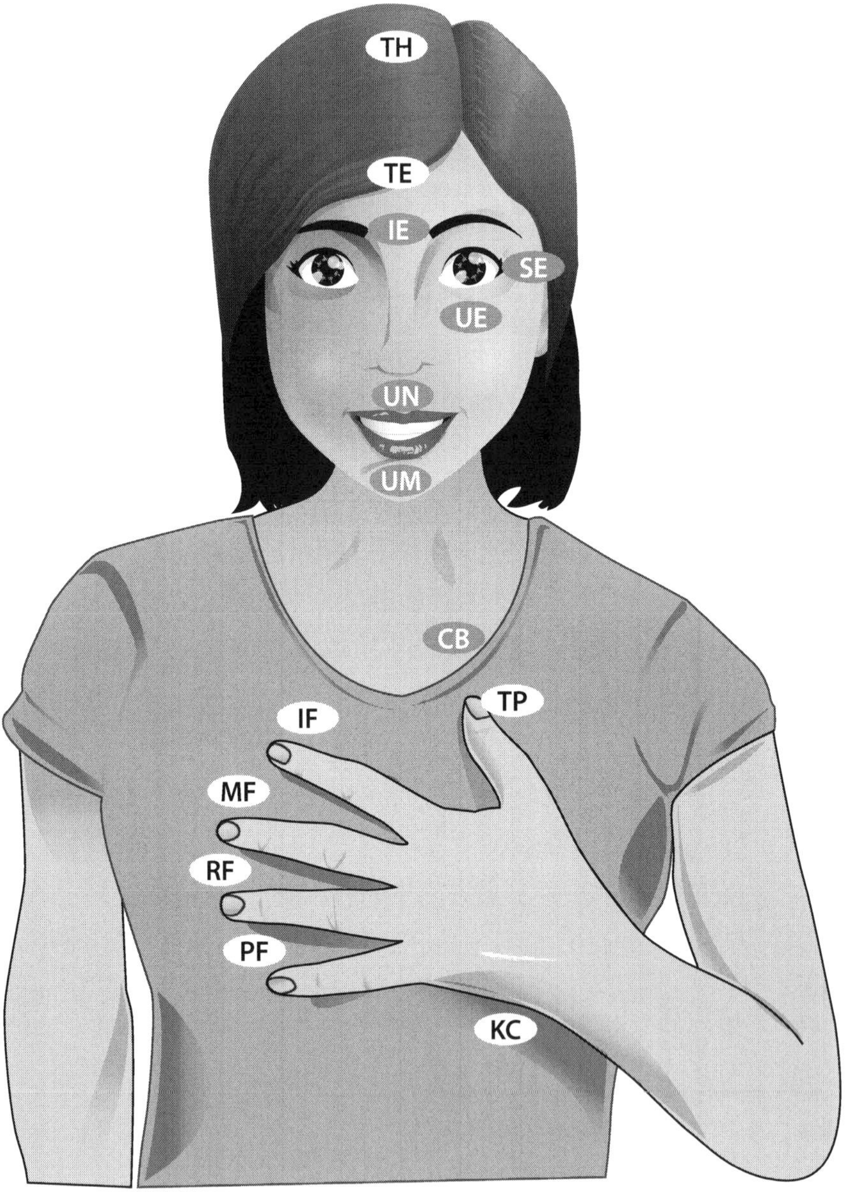
TH
TE
IE
SE
UE
UN
UM
CB
TP
IF
MF
RF
PF
KC

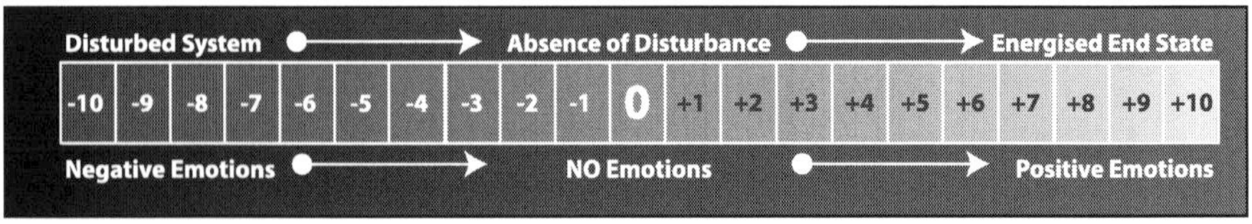
Disturbed System
Absence of Disturbance
Energised End State
-10 -9 -8 -7 -6 -5 -4 -3 -2 -1 0 +1 +2 +3 +4 +5 +6 +7 +8 +9 +10
Negative Emotions
NO Emotions
Positive Emotions

Here are some positive words to help you do a round of positive tapping: happy, friendship, love, laughter, hug, energy, inspiration, success, positive, creative, luck, joy, magic, health, sunshine, light, harmony, satisfaction, awesome, miracle, trust, clarity, fun, wonder, mystery, excitement, beauty, vision, future, angel, freedom, kindness, respect, hope, focus, drive, desire, and ambition.

Give this next round of tapping a title such as 'Feeling Happy' or 'Happy Energy' or 'Feeling Great'. This is your personal tapping session so tap using whatever positive emotions you want to feel or create, or just use the statements below.

Place your hands over your heart in the Heart Healing position, take three deep breaths and state your title. Now, tap through each of the points, starting at the top of your head and finishing on the karate chop point while using the statements associated with each point.

TH = Feeling happy.

TE = I feel so happy.

IE = Happy energy.

SE = Lots of happy energy.

UE = All this happy energy.

UN = Flowing through my body.

UM = Energy.

CB = Happy Energy.

TP = Feeling happy and relaxed.

IF = I feel so good.

MF = So chilled.

RF = So relaxed.

PF = All this happy energy.

KC = Feeling happy and energised.

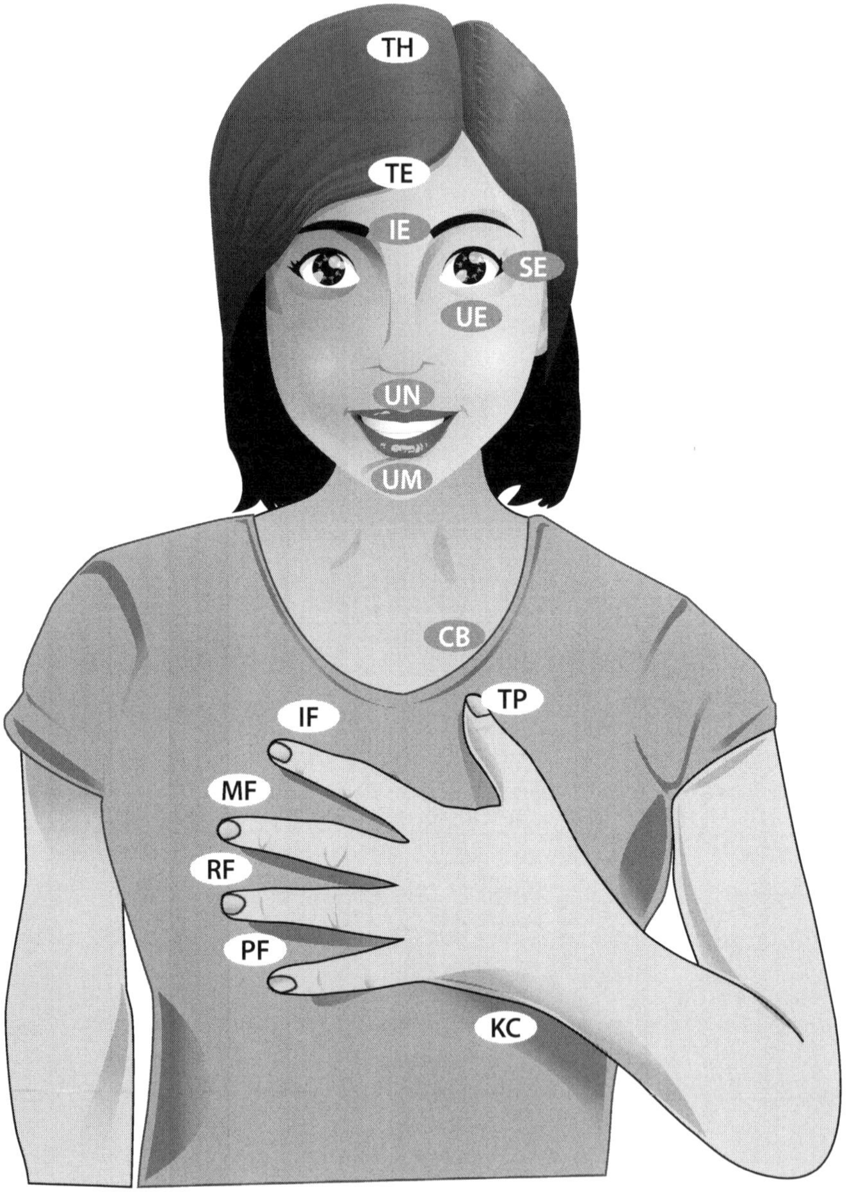
TH
TE
IE
SE
UE
UN
UM
CB
TP
IF
MF
RF
PF
KC

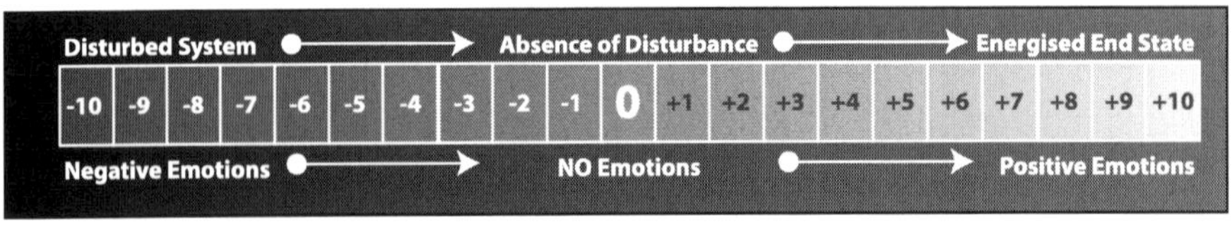
Disturbed System
Absence of Disturbance
Energised End State
-10 -9 -8 -7 -6 -5 -4 -3 -2 -1 0 +1 +2 +3 +4 +5 +6 +7 +8 +9 +10
Negative Emotions
NO Emotions
Positive Emotions

After you have tapped a positive round and taken three deep breaths with your hands over your heart in the Heart Healing position, look at the Tapping Scale again. Do you feel much better or happier now? Have your feelings improved? Has the number you originally chose gone to, say, a +3 or a +5?

You can continue to tap on, 'I feel really good' or 'I feel really positive' until you feel really good and have reached +5 or +6. If you reach a +10 you have experienced what is known as a healing event. You will feel amazing, like you could conquer the world. Teenagers have quite a sensitive energy system so you shouldn't need to do too many rounds before you are feeling well into the plus side of the Tapping Scale.

Test your progress by saying, 'I can read in front of the class now' or 'I am not scared anymore'. If you feel any resistance to this or you still feel a little bit scared, do a few more rounds of tapping to release any remaining negative emotions. Start with statements such as, 'I am still a little bit worried about reading in front of the class' or 'I am still a little worried the other students may laugh at me', and end with a positive statement such as, 'I have no problem reading in front of the class' or 'I can easily read in front of the class'. You will know when you are ready to read in front of the class when you no longer feel any negative emotions when you think about doing it.

HOW CAN TAPPING HELP YOU?

You can use tapping for so many things! It can help you in your everyday life, whether you need to concentrate on your school work or you need help to revise/study or release anxiety just before exams and tests. You can also tap to help with

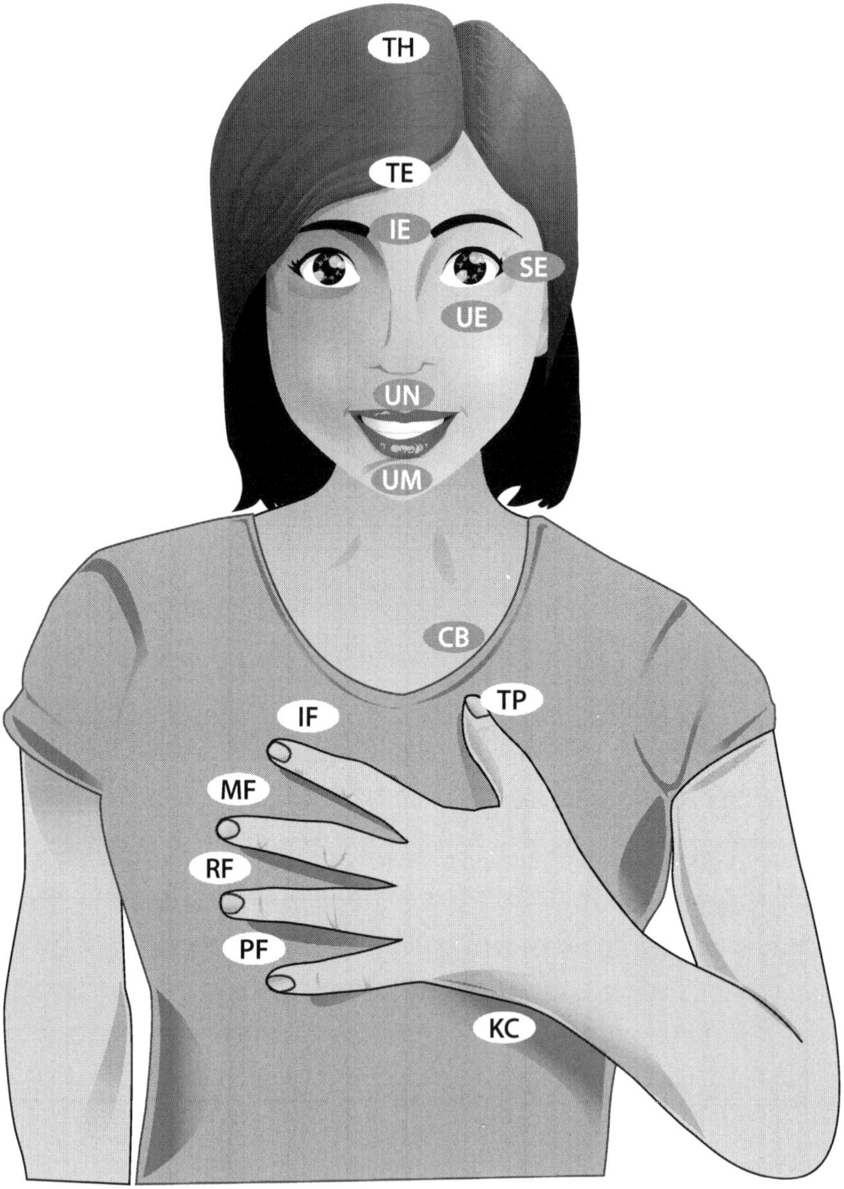
TH
TE
IE
SE
UE
UN
UM
CB
TP
IF
MF
RF
PF
KC

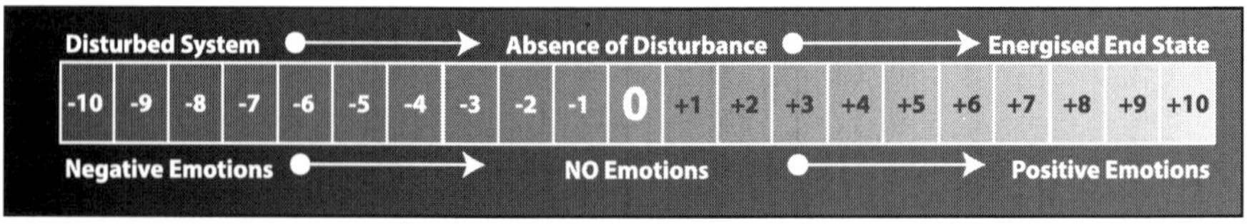
Disturbed System
Absence of Disturbance
Energised End State
-10 -9 -8 -7 -6 -5 -4 -3 -2 -1 0 +1 +2 +3 +4 +5 +6 +7 +8 +9 +10
Negative Emotions
NO Emotions
Positive Emotions

performance dealing with sports, to help you feel more confident, and feel less nervous or anxious so you can perform better.

Tapping can help you feel less anxious when you start a new school or go to the dentist. Even phobias like spiders, snakes, rats, etc., can be helped with tapping. Tapping also can help improve relationships with other teenagers, siblings, friends, teachers, parents or other adults by tapping away any feelings of anger, fear, frustration, jealousy, peer pressure, or bullying, etc.

More complex issues, like specific fears, abuse, self-harm, trauma, etc., are not covered in this book because these are better treated on a one-to-one basis with a qualified Energy EFT practitioner. The topics that are covered in this book should relieve to some extent the anxieties and fears related to any of the feelings previously mentioned.

TAPPING SCRIPTS FOR SPECIFIC PROBLEMS

Here are some tapping examples that may be relevant to how you are feeling now. Use tapping for any of them that you feel might help you or come back to any of them when you feel they will help you in the future.

Tapping to Reduce Anger

Anger and frustration are emotions that can affect teenagers on a regular basis. This next tapping sequence will help you to release some of these feelings and will give you a tool to use should you ever feel your anger is at a level where you need a bit of help to calm down.

Look at the Tapping Scale and pick a number that represents how you are feeling about an issue that makes you angry, such as a –4 or a –6. The worse you feel the lower the number will be.

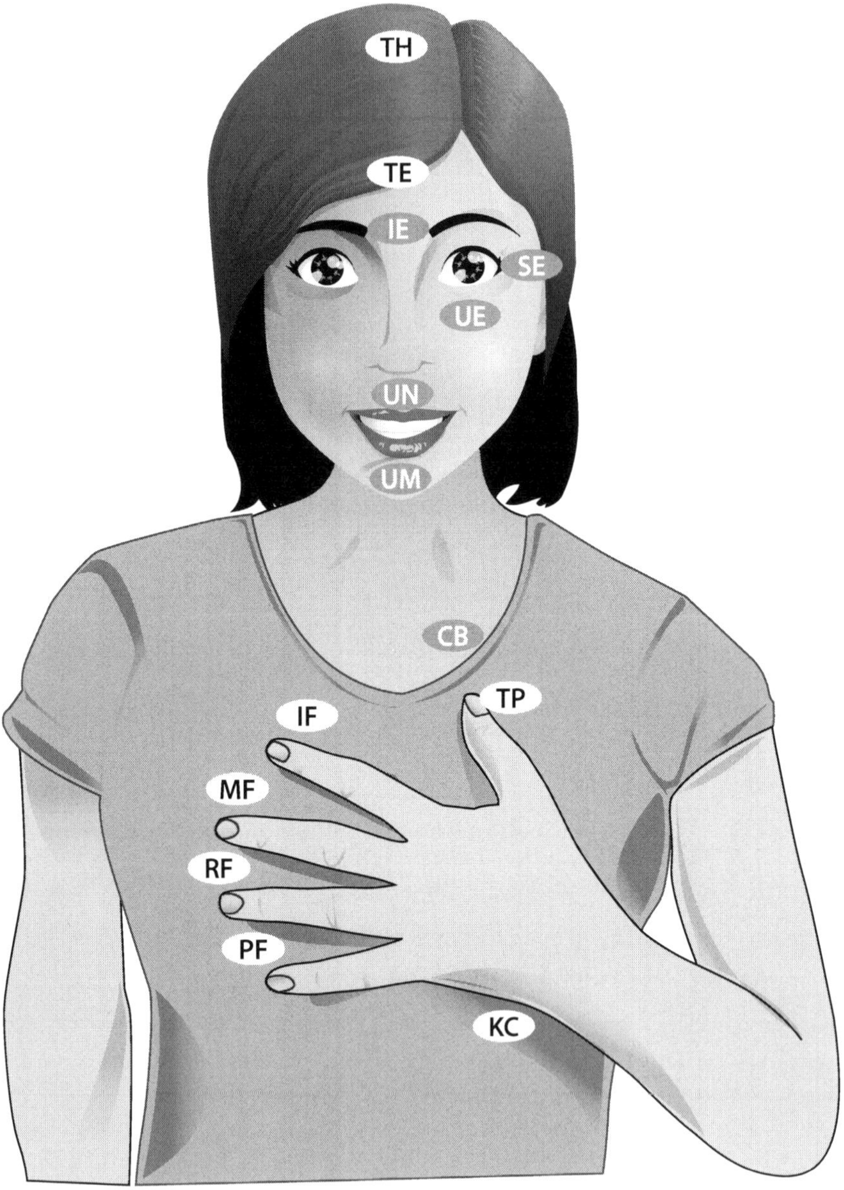
TH
TE
IE
SE
UE
UN
UM
CB
TP
IF
MF
RF
PF
KC

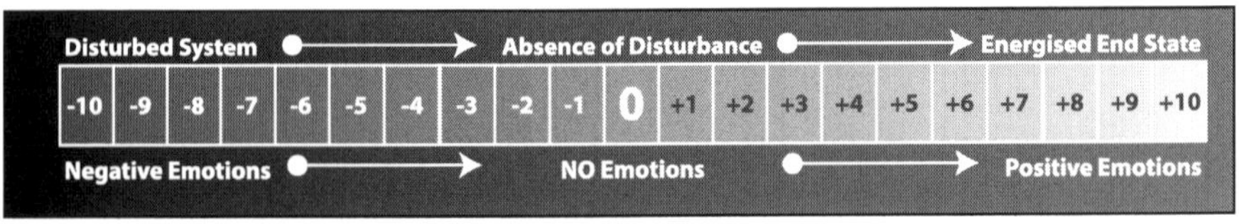
Disturbed System
Absence of Disturbance
Energised End State
-10 -9 -8 -7 -6 -5 -4 -3 -2 -1 0 +1 +2 +3 +4 +5 +6 +7 +8 +9 +10
Negative Emotions
NO Emotions
Positive Emotions

Give your problem a title, such as 'I Feel So Angry'. Place your hands over your heart in the Heart Healing position, take three deep breaths and state your title.

Now tap through all the points, starting at the top of the head and ending on the karate chop point. While you are tapping, say the statements in the following list related to each point or make up your own statements.

TH = Feeling really angry.

TE = All this anger in my body.

IE = Feeling so angry.

SE = I don't feel in control.

UE = I choose to release this anger.

UN = From every cell in my body.

UM = I choose to let it go.

CB = I choose to feel calm and confident.

TP = All this anger.

IF = This anger in my body.

MF = I choose to release it now.

RF = I choose to let it go.

PF = I release this anger into the universe.

KC = I choose to feel peaceful and relaxed.

Place your hands over your heart in the Heart Healing position and take three deep breaths. Measure how you feel now on the Tapping Scale. Has the level of your anger changed to, say, a –3, a –1, or even a zero?

Now tap another round through the points and change what you say in a way that will reflect your improved number.

TH = I still feel some of this anger.

TE = I feel so frustrated.

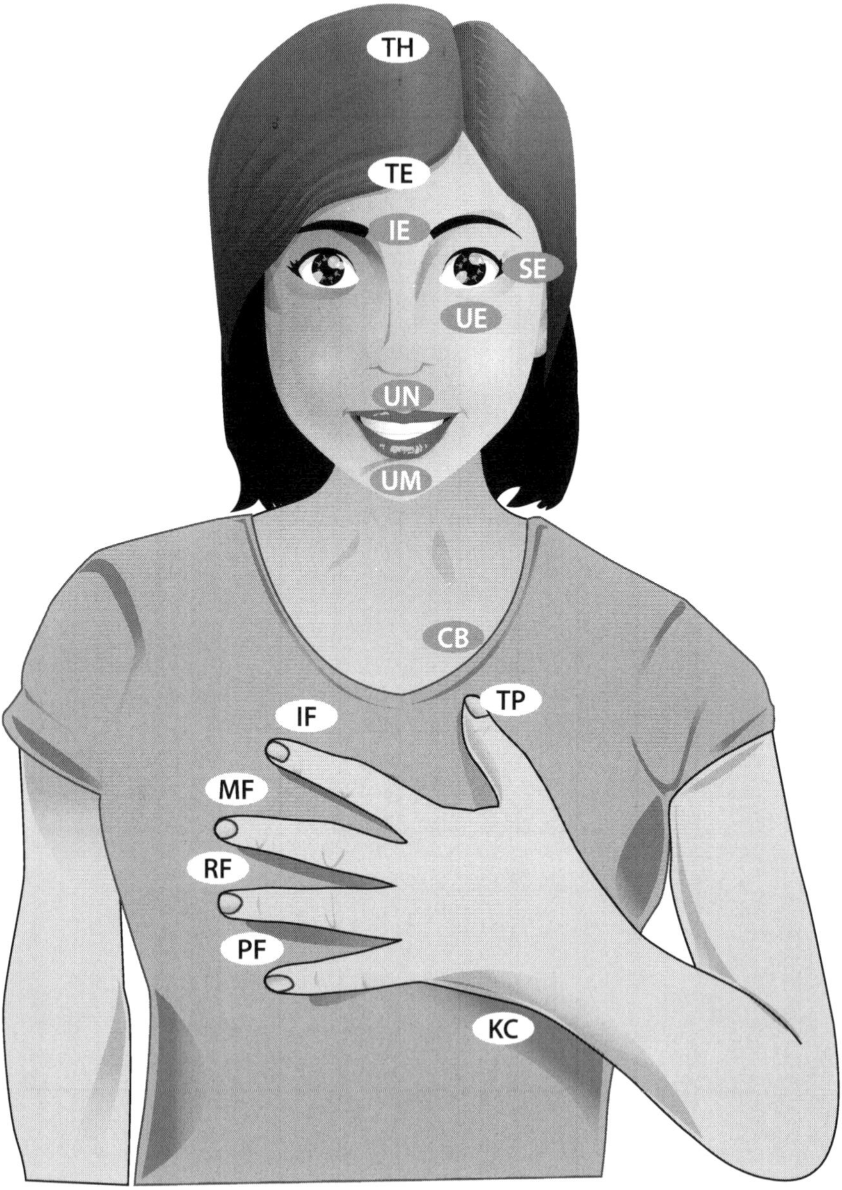
TH
TE
IE
SE
UE
UN
UM
CB
TP
IF
MF
RF
PF
KC

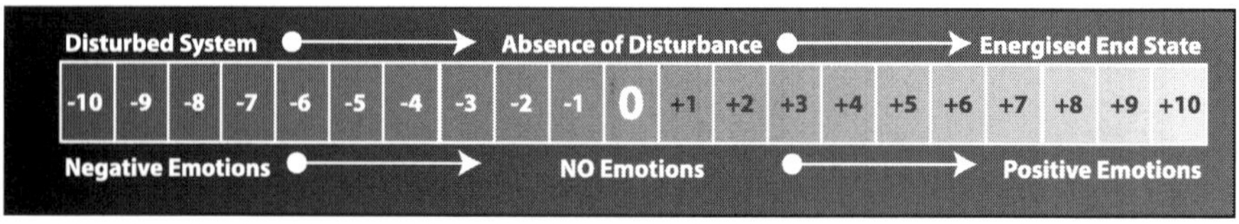
Disturbed System
Absence of Disturbance
Energised End State
-10 -9 -8 -7 -6 -5 -4 -3 -2 -1 0 +1 +2 +3 +4 +5 +6 +7 +8 +9 +10
Negative Emotions
NO Emotions
Positive Emotions

IE = No one listens to me.

SE = I choose to feel calm.

UE = I release all this anger.

UN = I choose to release it now.

UM = I choose to feel safe and protected.

CB = I choose to feel at peace.

TP = I choose to let go of this anger.

IF = Feeling happy and calm.

MF = I choose to feel in control.

RF = I release all this anger.

PF = I release this anger into the universe.

KC = I choose to feel safe and in control.

Place your hands over your heart in the Heart Healing position and take three deep breaths. Now measure how you feel on the Tapping Scale. Hopefully you are feeling better and have moved to, say, a +2 or even higher. If you still feel a little angry, tap another round through the points. However, if you feel more at peace, tap a happy, positive round. Give your emotions a new title, such as 'Feeling Happy' and use either the following statements or ones you create while you tap.

TH = Happy energy.

TE = All this happy energy.

IE = Flowing through my body.

SE = Feeling energised and relaxed.

UE = Helping me feel calm.

UN = Feeling energised.

UM = All this wonderful energy.

CB = Flowing through my body.

TP = Feeling peaceful and relaxed.

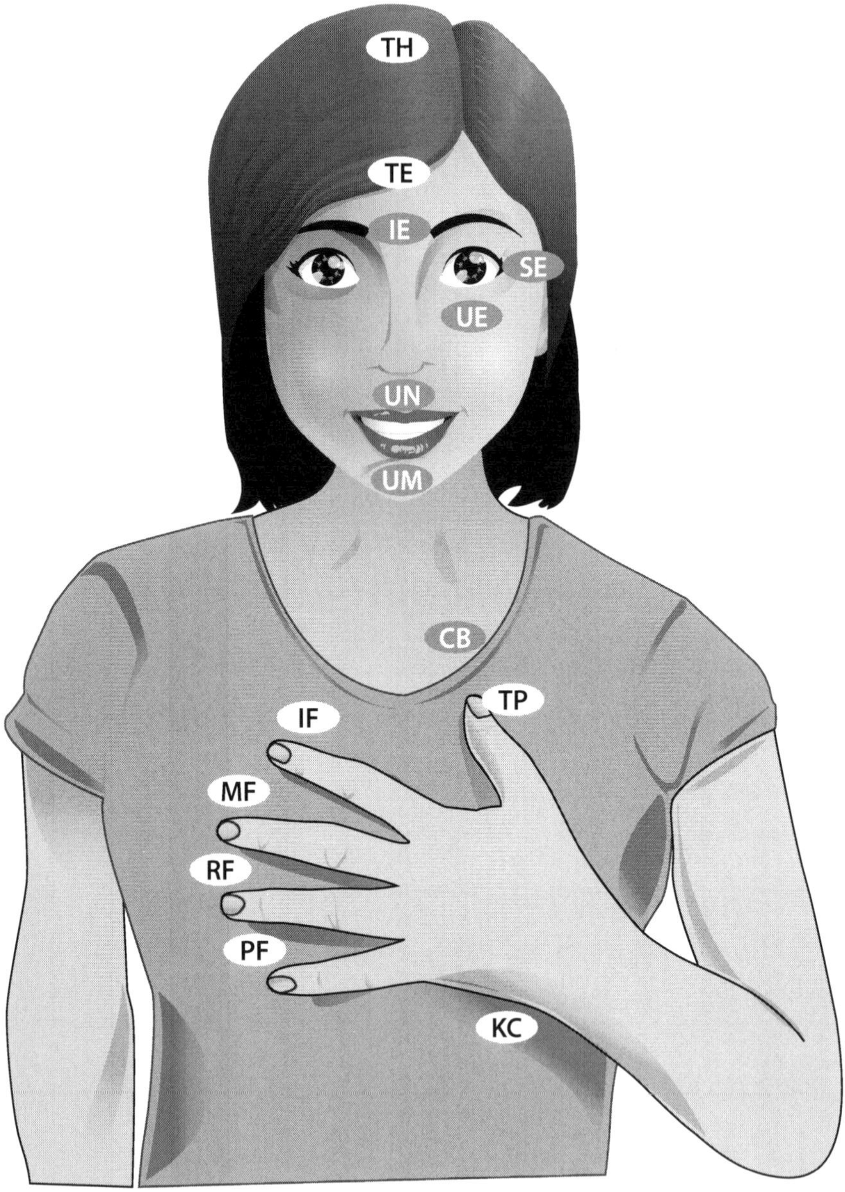
TH
TE
IE
SE
UE
UN
UM
CB
TP
IF
MF
RF
PF
KC

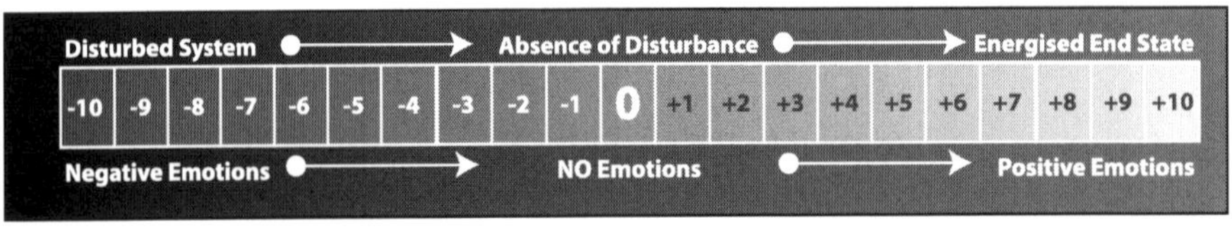
Disturbed System
Absence of Disturbance
Energised End State
-10 -9 -8 -7 -6 -5 -4 -3 -2 -1 0 +1 +2 +3 +4 +5 +6 +7 +8 +9 +10
Negative Emotions
NO Emotions
Positive Emotions

IF = Feeling safe and calm.

MF = Feeling happy and content.

RF = All this happy energy.

PF = Flowing through my body.

KC = I feel peaceful and protected.

Place your hands over your heart in the Heart Healing position and take three deep breaths.

Hopefully you are feeling happy and energised and on the plus side of the Tapping Scale. If you want to feel better still, tap another round using this sequence or add in additional words that will make you feel even better, such as love, sunshine or joy.

Tapping to Reduce Anxiety

Anxiety occurs in many teenagers' lives. Even the ones who feel confident most of the time can feel anxious when they are starting a new school, when exams are approaching or if they are trying something new. It is how you learn to manage your anxieties that makes all the difference to your life. Energy EFT is a wonderful tool that can really help to reduce your anxieties and to stay calm when the need arises.

Give your level of anxiety a number on the Tapping Scale, say a –4 or –6, or whatever number comes up for you depending on how anxious you are feeling.

Choose your title, such as 'Feeling Anxious'. Place your hands over your heart in the Heart Healing position, take three deep breaths and state your title. Now tap through all the points while you say either the following statements or ones you have created.

TH = Feeling anxious.

TE = All this anxiety in my body.

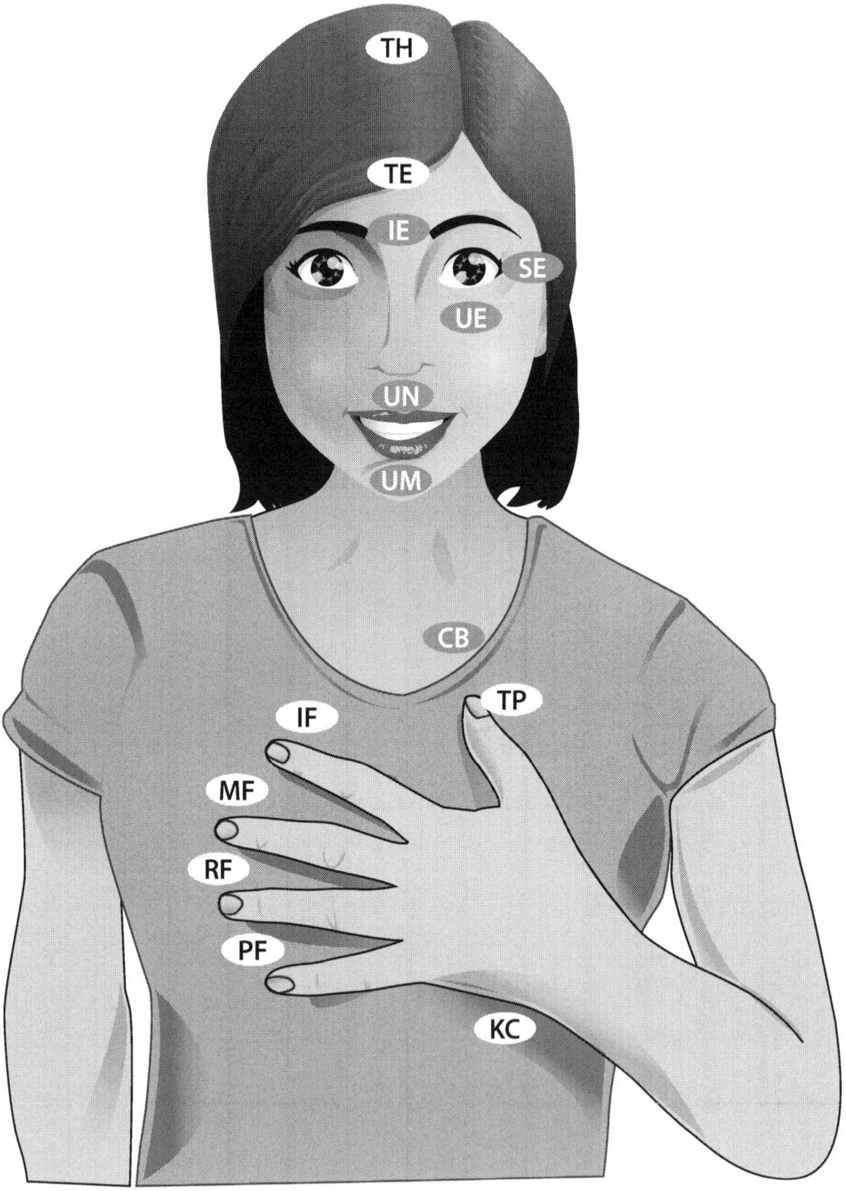
TH
TE
IE
SE
UE
UN
UM
CB
TP
IF
MF
RF
PF
KC

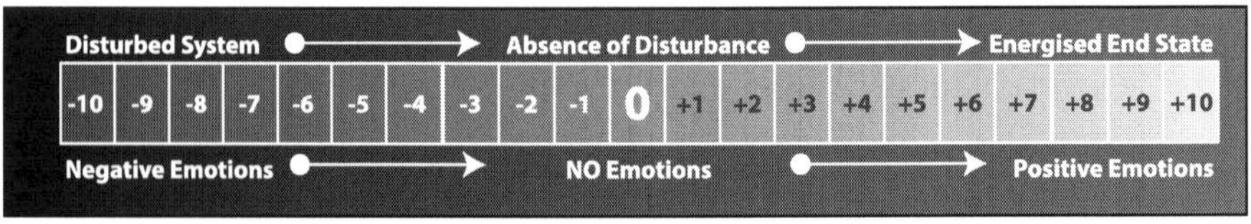
Disturbed System
Absence of Disturbance
Energised End State
-10 -9 -8 -7 -6 -5 -4 -3 -2 -1 0 +1 +2 +3 +4 +5 +6 +7 +8 +9 +10
Negative Emotions
NO Emotions
Positive Emotions

IE = All these anxious feelings.

SE = All this anxiety.

UE = I choose to release it now.

UN = From every cell of my body.

UM = I choose to let it go.

CB = All this anxiety.

TP = Flowing through my body.

IF = I choose to release it now.

MF = I release this anxiety.

RF = Feeling safe and protected.

PF = Letting go of this anxiety.

KC = Feeling calm and at peace.

Place your hands over your heart in the Heart Healing position and take three deep breaths. Notice how you feel now. Do you feel much calmer? Has the number on the Tapping Scale improved? You may want to repeat the sequence a few more times so you feel really calm and relaxed.

Once you have moved into the positive numbers, tap a happy round to feel even better.

Give this new round a title such as 'Feeling Good' and tap on all the points while using the suggested following statements.

TH = Feeling good.

TE = Feeling happy.

IE = Feeling really happy.

SE = Happy energy.

UE = All this happy energy.

UN = Flowing through my body.

UM = Happy feelings.

CB = Happy thoughts.

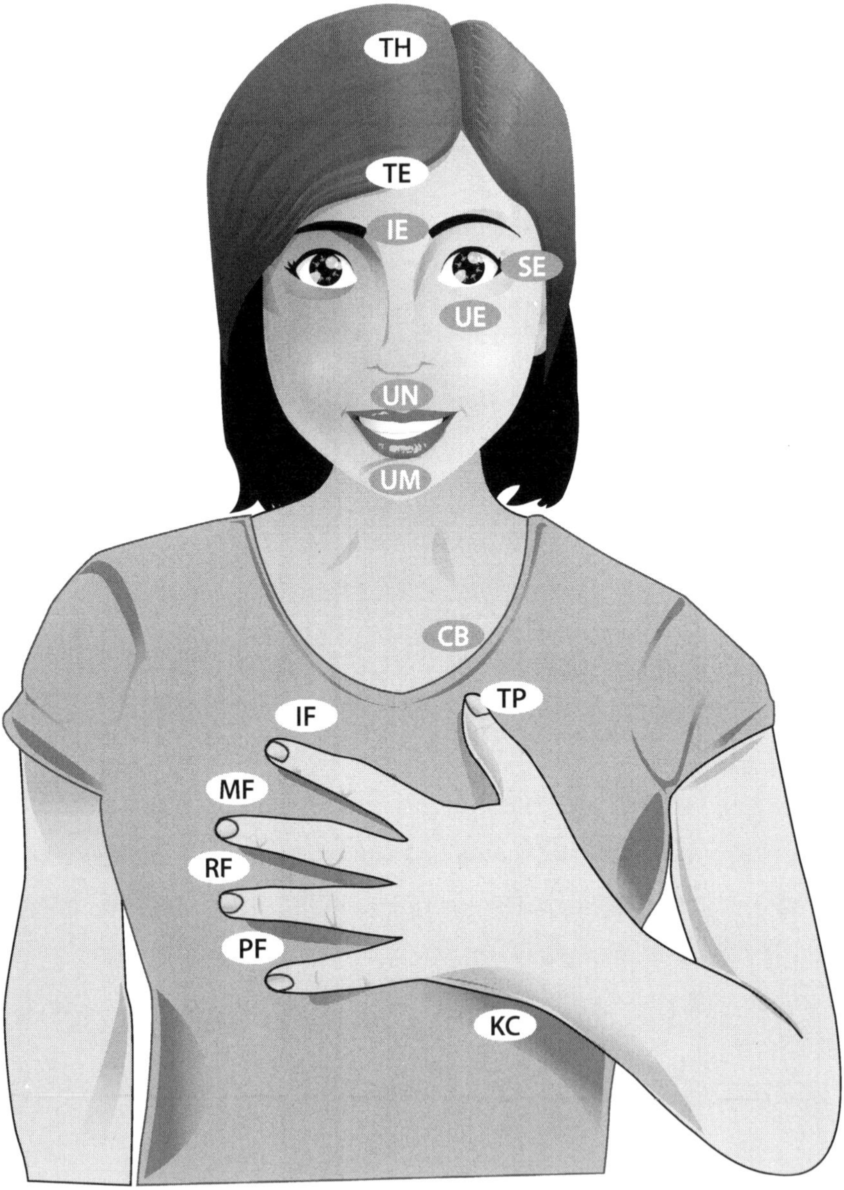
TH
TE
IE
SE
UE
UN
UM
CB
TP
IF
MF
RF
PF
KC

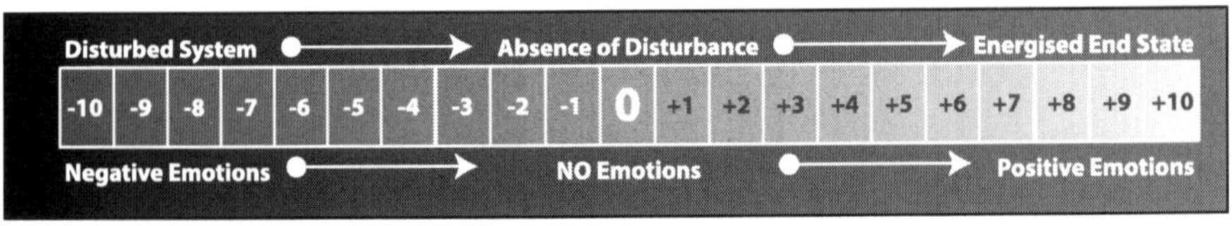
Disturbed System
Absence of Disturbance
Energised End State
-10 -9 -8 -7 -6 -5 -4 -3 -2 -1 0 +1 +2 +3 +4 +5 +6 +7 +8 +9 +10
Negative Emotions
NO Emotions
Positive Emotions

TP = Happiness.

IF = Feeling so happy.

MF = All this happiness.

RF = Wow, I feel amazing.

PF = Happy and energetic.

KC = Peaceful and content.

Place your hands over your heart in the Heart Healing position and take three deep breaths. Check the Tapping Scale again to see how much better you feel. Do a few more rounds if you need to but hopefully you are feeling refreshed and energised.

Tapping to Relieve Stress

Stress seems to affect everyone in the fast modern world we live in. Throughout school life and beyond everyone has challenges to face and targets they are expected to meet that can cause them to experience different levels of stress.

The most important thing is how you manage your stress. Life can be much easier if you can work with and recognise your stresses as they come into your life. Energy EFT is a simple, effective way to help reduce your stress levels when you are facing challenges in life, at home or at school.

Look at the Tapping Scale and choose a number that represents how stressed you are feeling. If you are feeling really stressed then you may be around a –4 or a –6. Give your problem a title, such as 'All This Stress'.

Place your hands over your heart in the Heart Healing position, take three deep breaths and state your title. While you are performing the tapping sequence, use the following statements or ones you create.

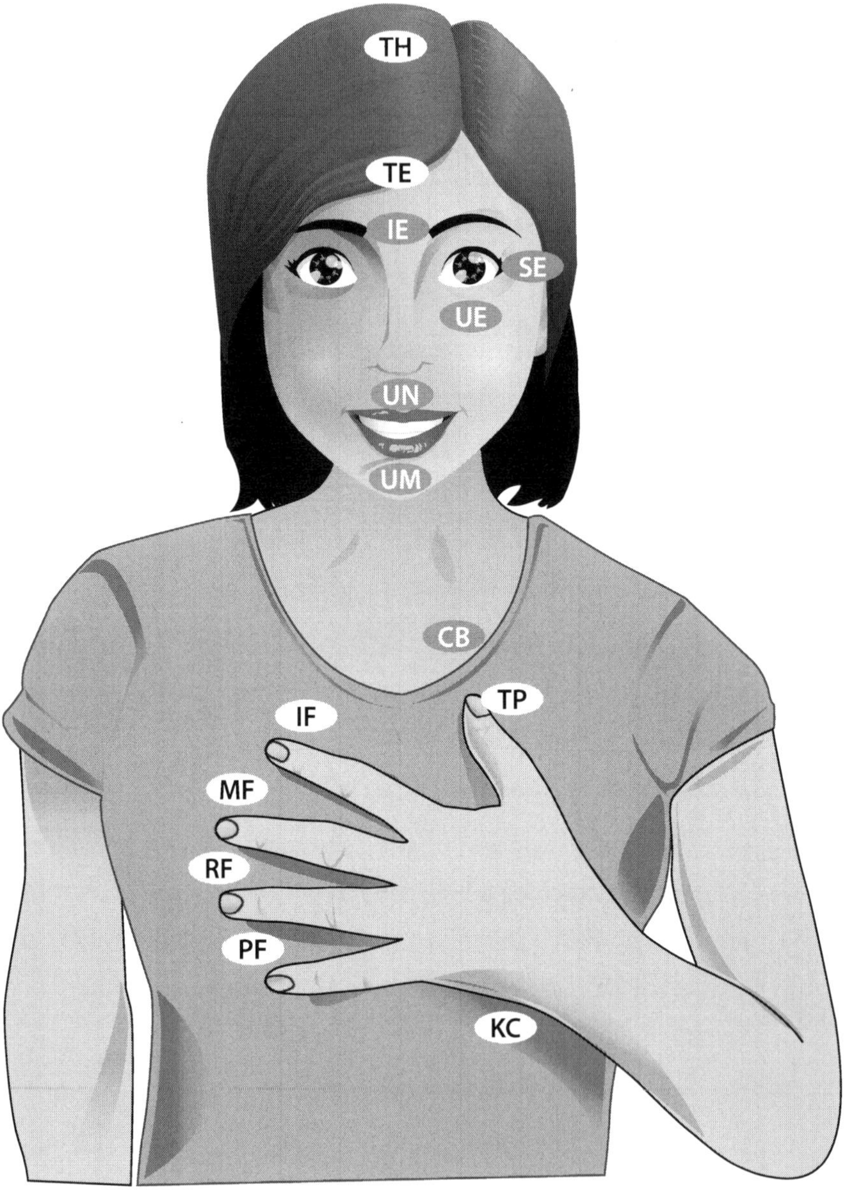
TH
TE
IE
SE
UE
UN
UM
CB
TP
IF
MF
RF
PF
KC

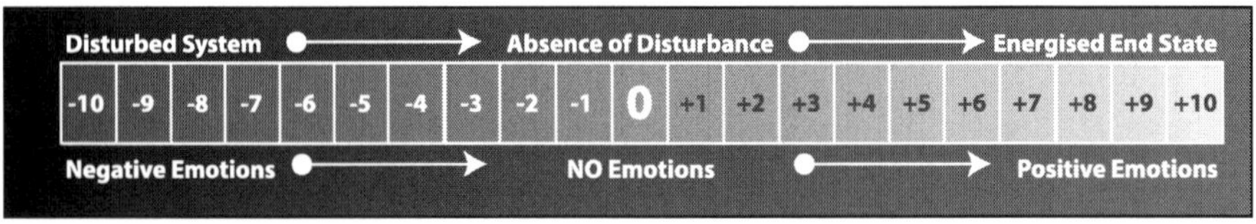
Disturbed System
Absence of Disturbance
Energised End State
-10 -9 -8 -7 -6 -5 -4 -3 -2 -1 0 +1 +2 +3 +4 +5 +6 +7 +8 +9 +10
Negative Emotions
NO Emotions
Positive Emotions

TH = All this stress, I feel in my body.

TE = I am under so much stress.

IE = In every cell in my body.

SE = Making me feel so low.

UE = I feel like I can't cope.

UN = It's like a big black cloud hanging over me.

UM = I choose to let go of this stress.

CB = I choose to feel at peace.

TP = Letting go of all this stress.

IF = Releasing it from my body.

MF = I choose to let it go.

RF = I choose to feel calm and confident.

PF = Letting go of all this stress.

KC = I choose to feel in control.

Place your hands over your heart in the Heart Healing position and take three deep breaths. Has your stress changed for the better on the Tapping Scale? If you still feel a little stressed, tap another round.

Once you feel your stress number has improved, tap through a happy round to make you feel even better. Give this round a title such as 'Happy Energy'. Place your hands over your heart in the Heart Healing position and take three deep breaths and then state your chosen title. Now tap through all the points using the statements below, or ones that feel more right for you.

TH = Feeling happy.

TE = I feel so happy.

IE = Happy energy.

SE = Lots of happy energy.

UE = All this happy energy.

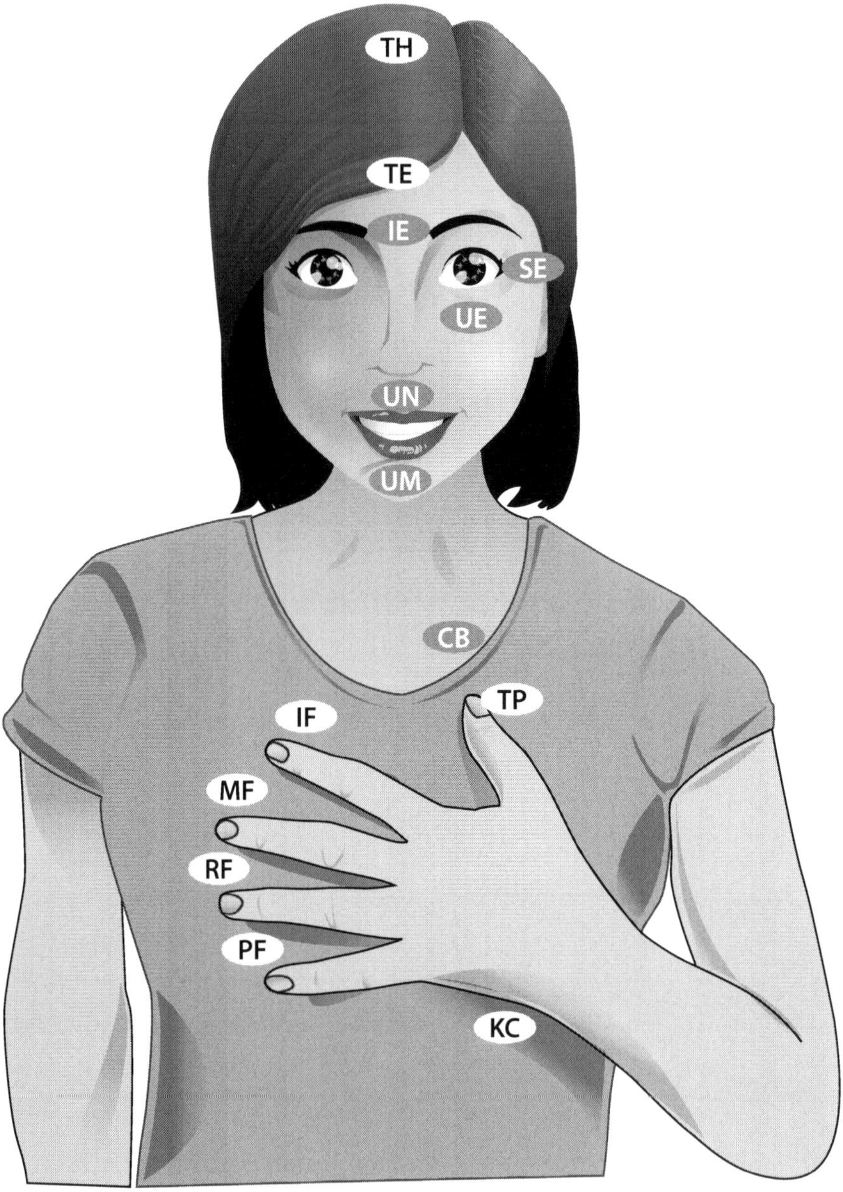
TH
TE
IE
SE
UE
UN
UM
CB
TP
IF
MF
RF
PF
KC

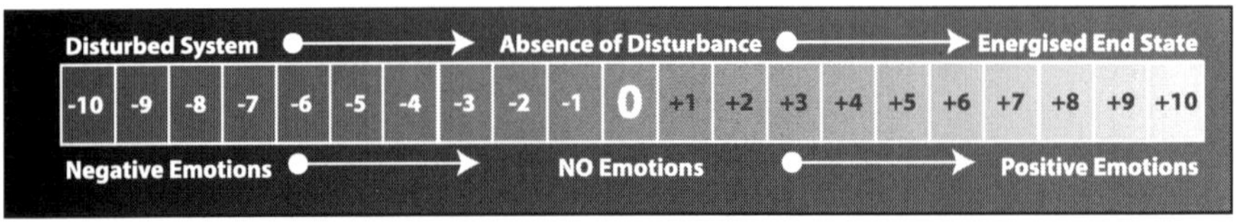
Disturbed System
Absence of Disturbance
Energised End State
-10 -9 -8 -7 -6 -5 -4 -3 -2 -1 0 +1 +2 +3 +4 +5 +6 +7 +8 +9 +10
Negative Emotions
NO Emotions
Positive Emotions

UN = Flowing through my body.

UM = Energy.

CB = Happy Energy.

TP = Feeling happy and relaxed.

IF = I feel so good.

MF = So chilled out.

RF = So relaxed.

PF = All this happy energy.

KC = Feeling happy and energised.

Place your hands over your heart in the Heart Healing position and take three deep breaths. If you feel you need to, repeat. Hopefully you are now on the plus side of the Tapping Scale and feeling great.

Tapping to Relieve Low Self-Esteem

Most people suffer from low self-esteem at some point in their lives. This could be because of a negative comment someone has made to them or they might have been teased or bullied. As a result, they can lose confidence in themselves and find it hard to deal with their emotions.

If you are dealing with low self-esteem, doing a few rounds of tapping can help to diminish or remove these negative feelings and you will have a good grounding for moving forward with a more positive outlook on life.

Check on the Tapping Scale to determine how much your low self-esteem is affecting you. You may say a –4 or a –5.

Give your feelings a title such as, ‘Feeling Really Low’. Place your hands over your heart in the Heart Healing position, take three deep breaths and state your title. Now tap a round while using the following statements or ones you devise.

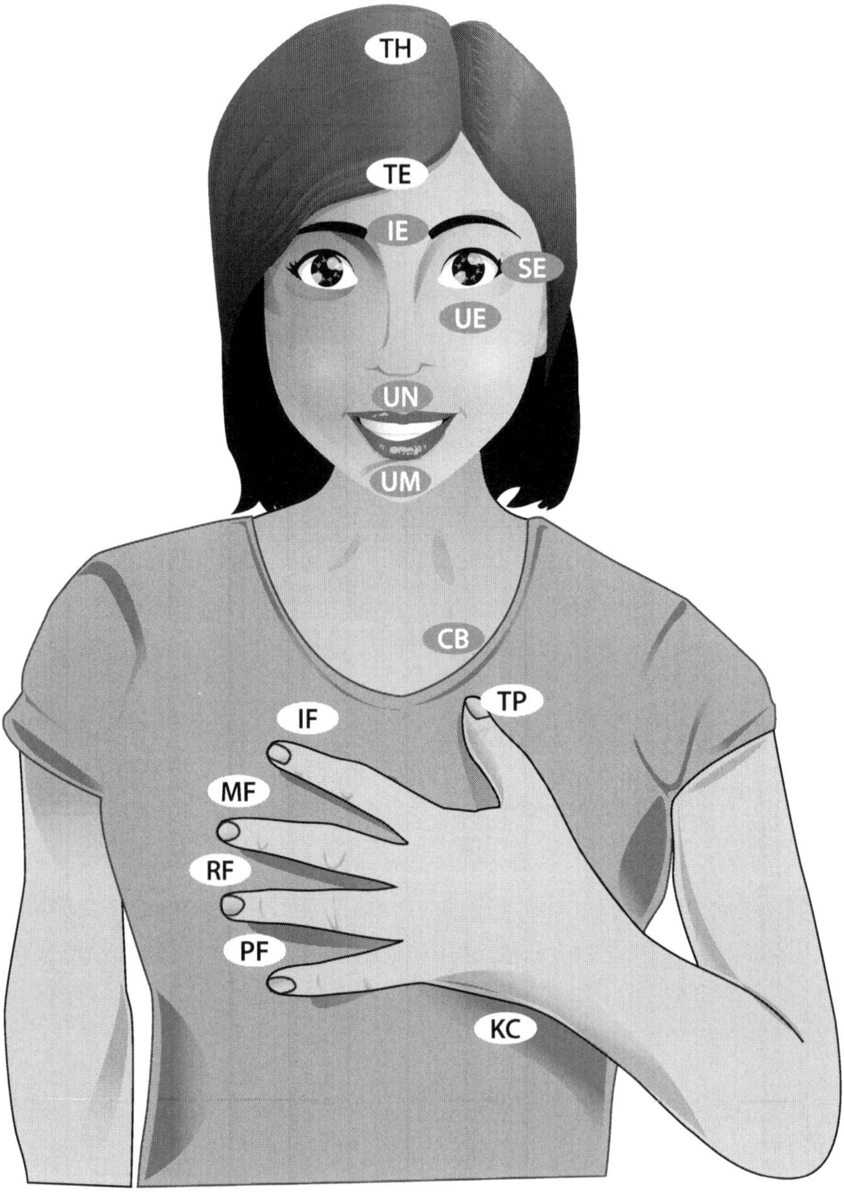
TH
TE
IE
SE
UE
UN
UM
CB
TP
IF
MF
RF
PF
KC

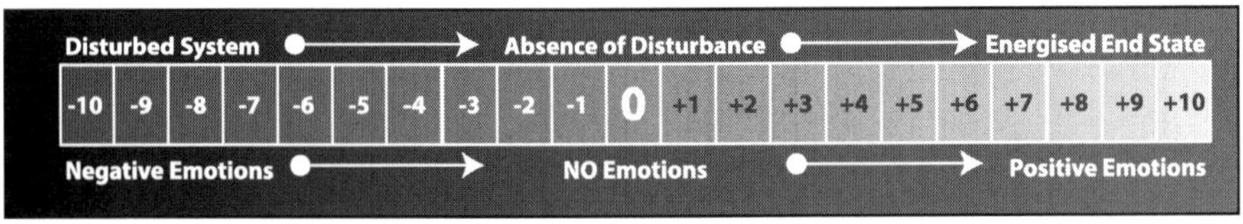
Disturbed System
Absence of Disturbance
Energised End State
-10 -9 -8 -7 -6 -5 -4 -3 -2 -1 0 +1 +2 +3 +4 +5 +6 +7 +8 +9 +10
Negative Emotions
NO Emotions
Positive Emotions

TH = Feeling really low.

TE = No confidence in myself.

IE = I can't do anything right.

SE = Feeling low and undervalued.

UE = Feeling useless and unloved.

UN = I feel like no one cares.

UM = Feeling really sad.

CB = Feeling so unhappy.

TP = I choose to take control.

IF = I choose to feel worthy of love.

MF = I choose to feel happy and confident.

RF = Releasing all this negativity.

PF = Feeling calm and confident.

KC = Feeling safe and protected.

Place your hands over your heart in the Heart Healing position and take three deep breaths. Let all the negativity go. Check your progress on the Tapping Scale. Do you feel a little better? You may have gone from, say, a –4 to a –2, or you may feel neutral at a zero. If you still feel low, tap a few more rounds until you are at zero or a +1 or +2.

Once you are feeling better, do a happy, positive round of tapping. Choose a title such as 'Feeling Good About Myself'. Place your hands over your heart in the Heart Healing position, take three deep breaths and state your title. Tap through all of the points while repeating the following statements associated with each point or create your own.

TH = Feeling happy and content.

TE = I am worthy of love and kindness.

IE = I am awesome.

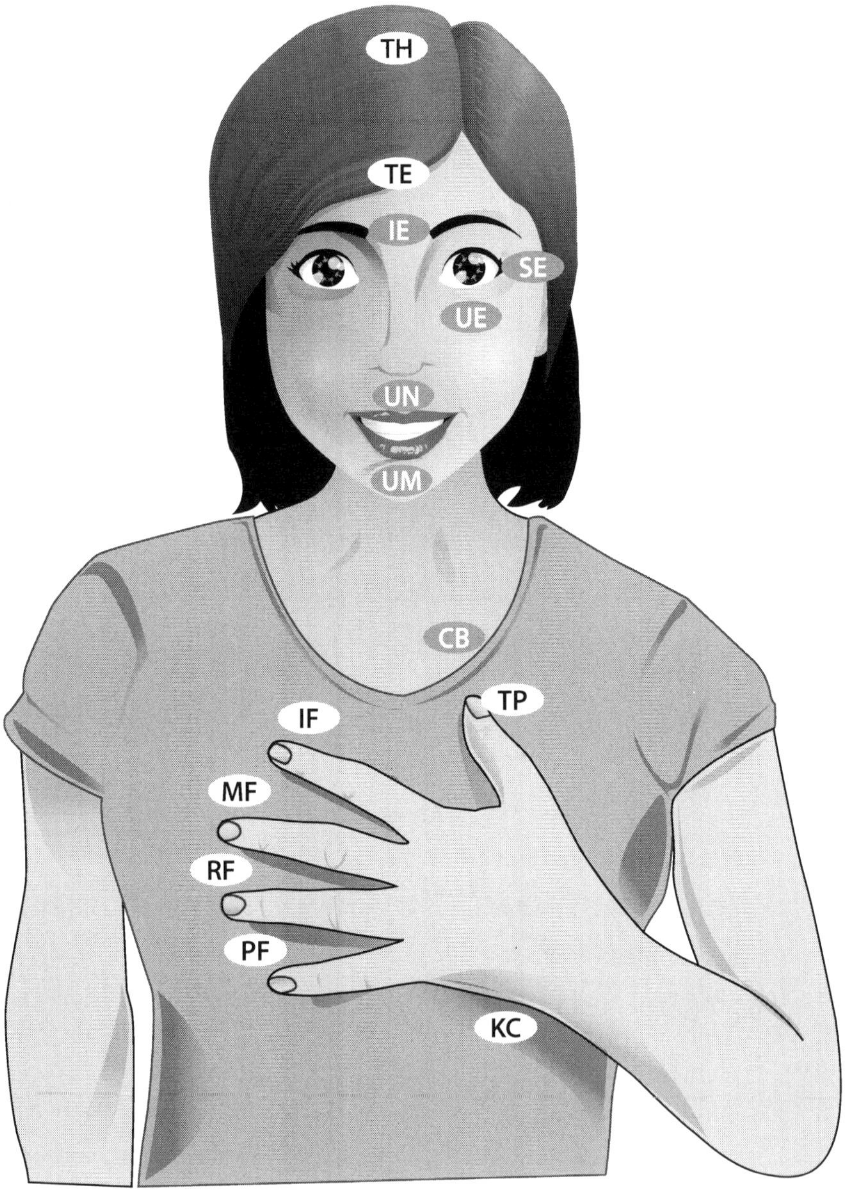
TH
TE
IE
SE
UE
UN
UM
CB
TP
IF
MF
RF
PF
KC

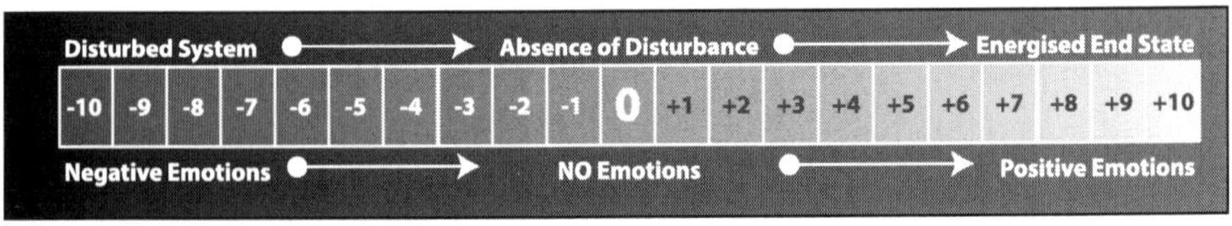
Disturbed System
Absence of Disturbance
Energised End State
-10 -9 -8 -7 -6 -5 -4 -3 -2 -1 0 +1 +2 +3 +4 +5 +6 +7 +8 +9 +10
Negative Emotions
NO Emotions
Positive Emotions

SE = I deserve to be heard.

UE = I deserve to be noticed.

UN = Feeling happy and protected.

UM = Safe and relaxed.

CB = I start my positive journey.

TP = I surround myself with happiness.

IF = I am enough.

MF = I am worthy of good things.

RF = Just watch me shine.

PF = Feeling safe and protected.

KC = Happy and content.

When you are done, place your hands over your heart in the Heart Healing position and take three deep breaths to release any negative feelings. Repeat a round if you need to. Check your progress on the Tapping Scale and hopefully you are feeling much better and on the plus side.

Tapping to Relieve Exam or Test Nerves

Exam or test nerves affect most students at some point in their school, college or university lives. Tapping is an excellent tool to help reduce the anxiety and pressure around the time of exams or tests. Releasing the pressure, stress or anxiety enables students to concentrate more easily on the task they are trying to perform. A good time to tap would be before you revise/study, or on the night before an exam, so you can concentrate and not get too overwhelmed by it all. You can also tap just before an exam if you get the chance to do so. Discreetly hold or massage the points if you are embarrassed anyone will see what you are doing.

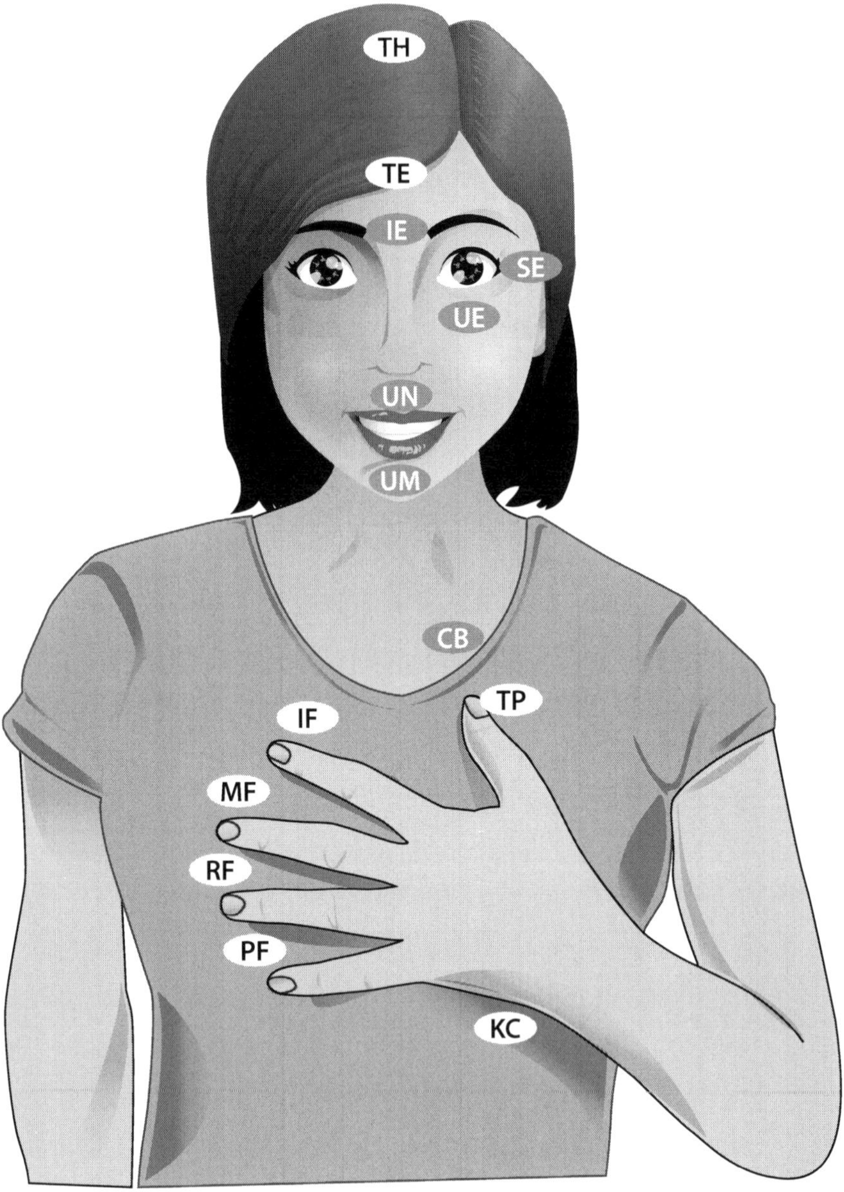
TH
TE
IE
SE
UE
UN
UM
CB
TP
IF
MF
RF
PF
KC

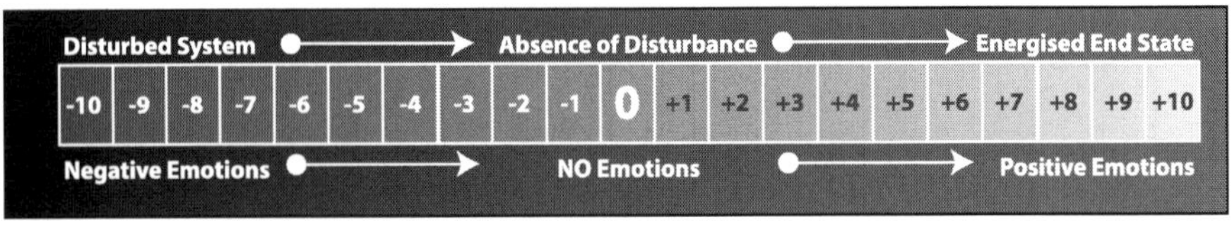
Disturbed System
Absence of Disturbance
Energised End State
-10 -9 -8 -7 -6 -5 -4 -3 -2 -1 0 +1 +2 +3 +4 +5 +6 +7 +8 +9 +10
Negative Emotions
NO Emotions
Positive Emotions

Choose your level of stress or anxiety on the Tapping Scale. It might be a –4 or a –5. Give your stress level a title, such as 'These Exams Are Making Me So Stressed'.

Place your hands over your heart in the Heart Healing position, take three deep breaths and state your title. Now tap through all the points while using either the following statements or statements of your own.

TH = Feeling so stressed.

TE = All this pressure to perform.

IE = Feeling really anxious.

SE = This revision/studying is never ending.

UE = I feel like I can't function.

UN = My head is full of stress.

UM = I feel like I'm in a fog.

CB = I feel so overwhelmed.

TP = I choose to release these feelings now.

IF = I choose to feel calm and confident.

MF = I can be productive in my work.

RF = I choose to release this pressure.

PF = I choose to feel peaceful and relaxed.

KC = I am doing my best to succeed.

Place your hands over your heart in the Heart Healing position and take three deep breaths. How do you feel now? Do you feel a little lighter? Less stressed? Has the number on the Tapping Scale gone to, say, a –1 or a zero?

Do a few more rounds until you feel like you are at zero or rising into the plus numbers on the Tapping Scale.

Once you are feeling better, do a happy, positive round of tapping. Choose a title such as 'Feeling Confident'. Place your

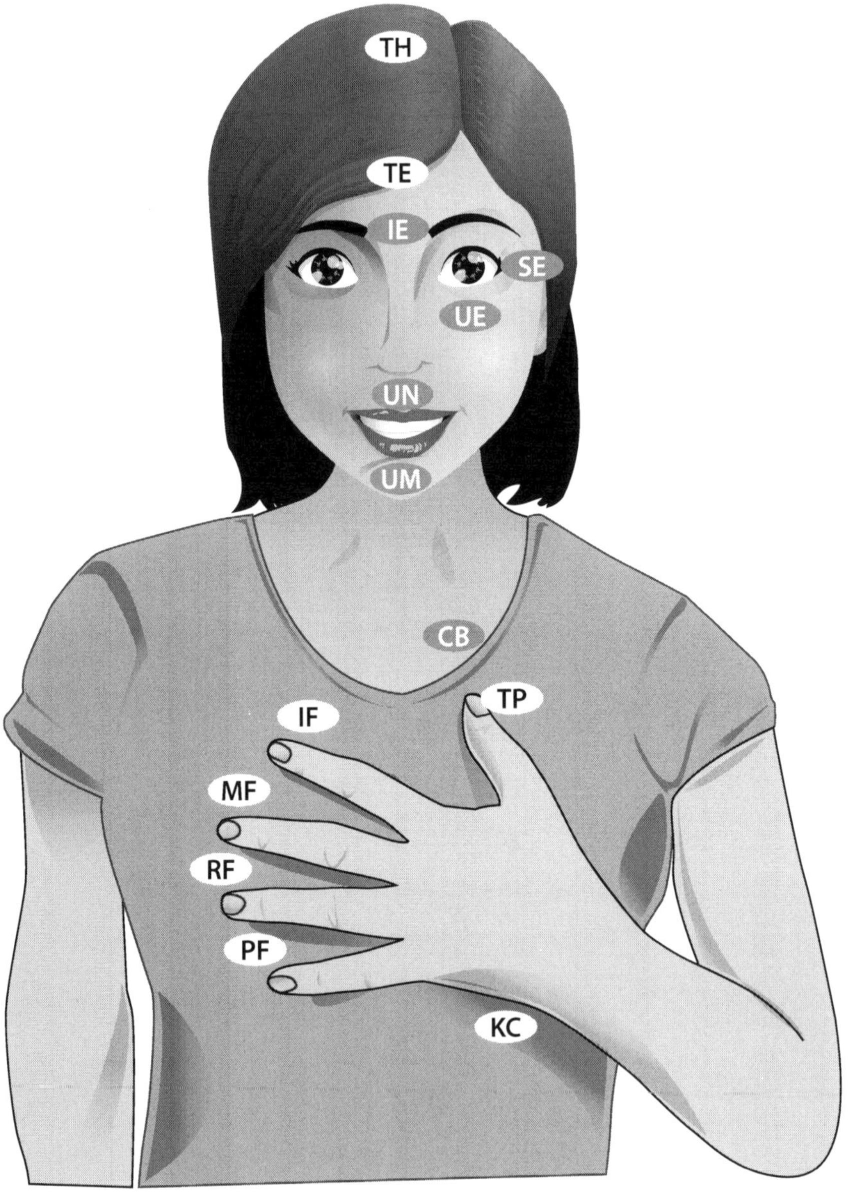
TH
TE
IE
SE
UE
UN
UM
CB
TP
IF
MF
RF
PF
KC

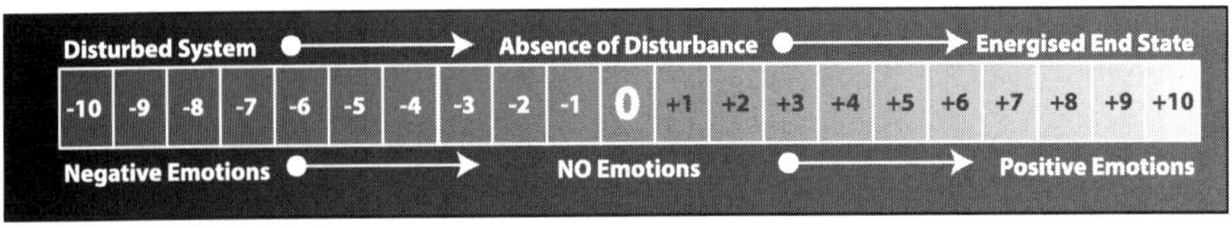
Disturbed System
Absence of Disturbance
Energised End State
-10 -9 -8 -7 -6 -5 -4 -3 -2 -1 0 +1 +2 +3 +4 +5 +6 +7 +8 +9 +10
Negative Emotions
NO Emotions
Positive Emotions

hands over your heart in the Heart Healing position, take three deep breaths and state your title. Tap through all of the points while repeating the following statements associated with each point or create your own.

TH = I will try my hardest to succeed.

TE = I know I can do this.

IE = I give myself permission to relax.

SE = I choose to feel calm and confident.

UE = I will try to the best of my ability.

UN = I am ready to take up the challenge.

UM = I choose to take the pressure off myself.

CB = I choose to relax and let it flow.

TP = It's going to be okay.

IF = My anxiety is lifting.

MF = I feel relaxed and confident.

RF = I feel safe and secure.

PF = Calm and peaceful.

KC = Ready to take control.

Place your hands over your heart in the Heart Healing position, take three deep breaths and let any remaining anxiety go. Hopefully by now you will be feeling a bit more confident and will be better prepared to revise/study or take your exams.

Tapping to Improve Self-Image and Body Confidence

Ask any teenager if they are happy with themselves and their body and most of them will say no. The comments will include, but are not limited to, my bum is too big, my boobs are too small or too big, my muscles are too weak, I'm too short or too tall, I've got a big nose, or I have a big chin or big ears. The list is endless.

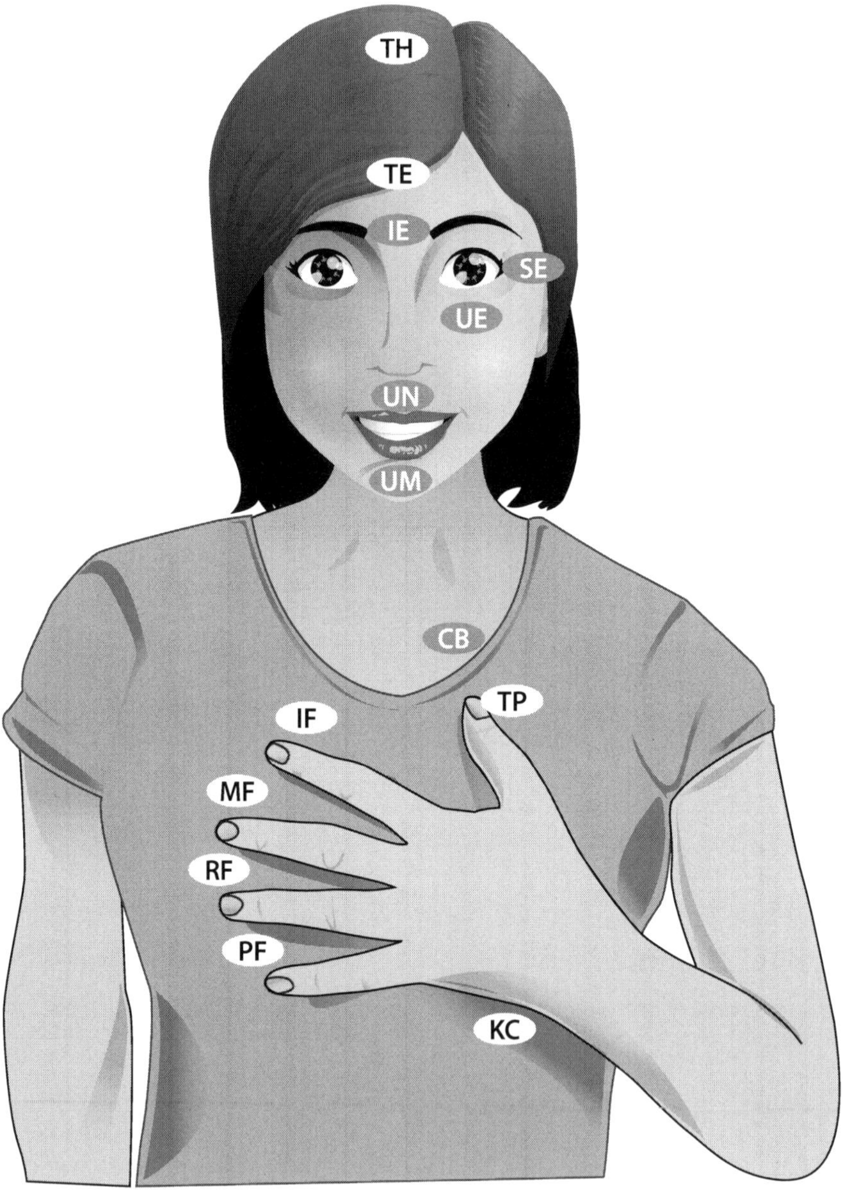
TH
TE
IE
SE
UE
UN
UM
CB
TP
IF
MF
RF
PF
KC

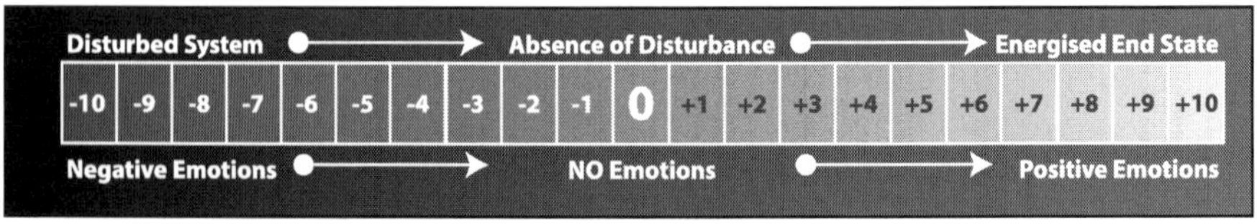
Disturbed System
Absence of Disturbance
Energised End State
-10 -9 -8 -7 -6 -5 -4 -3 -2 -1 0 +1 +2 +3 +4 +5 +6 +7 +8 +9 +10
Negative Emotions
NO Emotions
Positive Emotions

Puberty and the teenage years can be awkward for both boys and girls for a multitude of reasons. This is when a cocktail of hormones is racing around their bodies that they don't have a clue how to control. Add in pressures at home, school and with their peers, and it's no wonder teenagers have difficulty coping.

Developing into a grown-up is tough. Teenagers can develop spots or acne, boys' voices break, boys grow facial and both boys and girls grow body hair, features grow and change, and bodies change and develop into the adult form almost overnight.

Learning to cope and to like or love yourself during this transition period will make the whole process much easier. Be kind to yourself. After all you would not be nearly as critical if you were telling a friend not to worry about his or her weight or any other changes that are going on with their body.

Sadly, some teenagers are teased about these changes which can cause them to be embarrassed or humiliated. This can lead to a lack of self-confidence and a poor body image.

Nearly everyone wants to fit in and feel normal. You are not alone in these emotions because most teenagers feel some form of self-doubt, even if you might think everyone is coping so much better than you are.

Energy EFT can be of great benefit during this period in your life. It can smooth out many of your worries and help you to feel a little more confident in yourself.

Look at the Tapping Scale and choose a number. If your body image or self-confidence is really low it will probably be a minus number, such as a –4 or a –5. Now, give how you feel a title, such as 'I Have No Confidence in the Way I Look'. Place your hands over your heart in the Heart Healing position, take three deep breaths and state your title. Now tap through all the points while using the following statements or statements of your own.

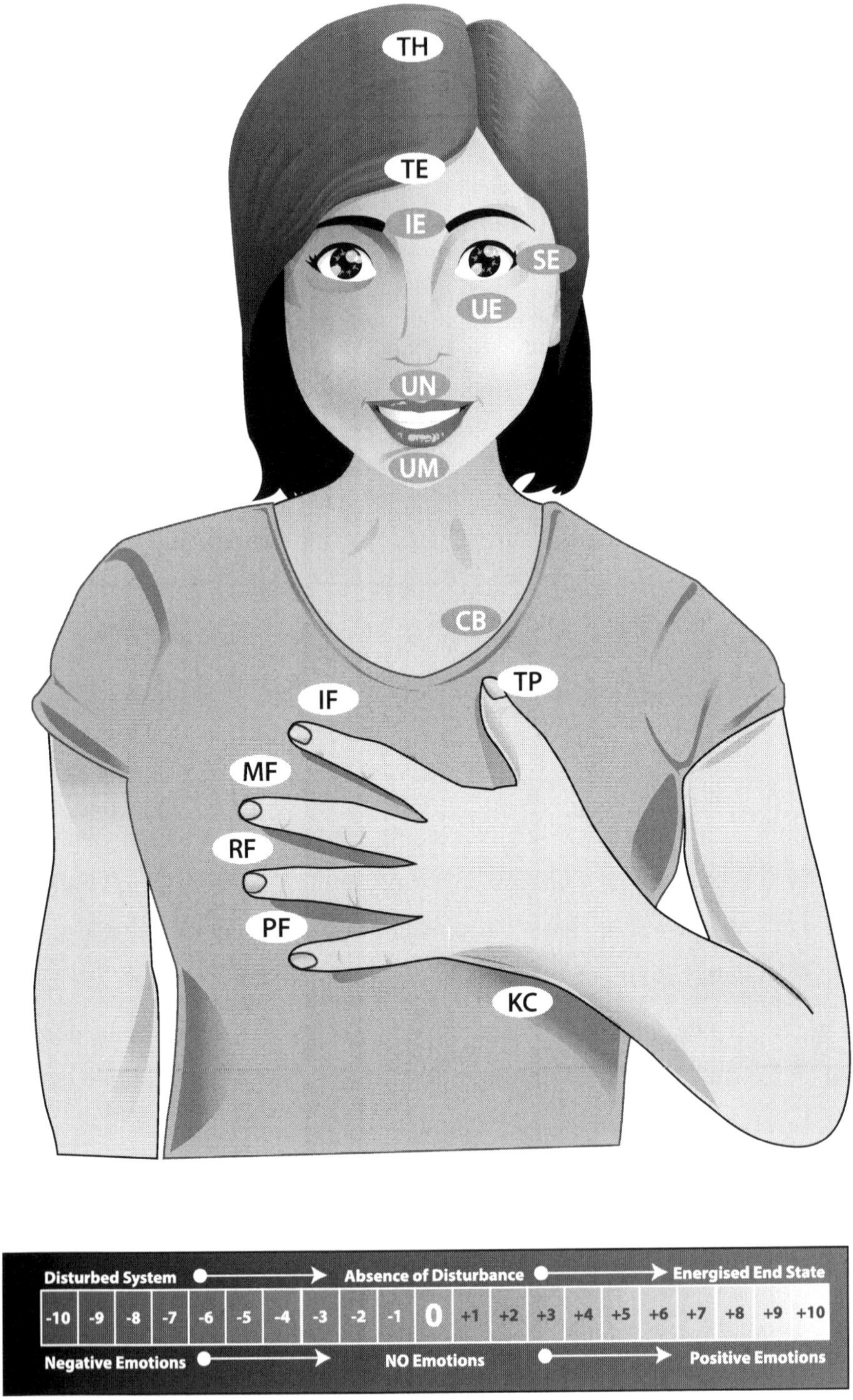
TH
TE
IE
SE
UE
UN
UM
CB
TP
IF
MF
RF
PF
KC
Disturbed System
Absence of Disturbance
Energised End State
-10 -9 -8 -7 -6 -5 -4 -3 -2 -1 0 +1 +2 +3 +4 +5 +6 +7 +8 +9 +10
Negative Emotions
NO Emotions
Positive Emotions

TH = I find it difficult to like myself.

TE = I feel embarrassed by the changes in my body.

IE = It is so hard growing up.

SE = It is really hard to fit in.

UE = All these changes in my body.

UN = I think everyone is better than me.

UM = I wish I could to learn to love and accept myself.

CB = I wish I could be confident with who I am.

TP = I am unique and I am okay.

IF = Maybe I could learn to be kind to myself?

MF = Maybe I could learn to love myself?

RF = I choose to feel confident in who I am.

PF = I choose to feel confident in my body.

KC = It is okay to be me.

Place your hands over your heart in the Heart Healing position and take three deep breaths. Has the number you chose on the Tapping Scale changed, going from, say, a –3 to a zero or perhaps into the plus numbers, such as to a +2? Do a few more rounds until you feel you can like, love or accept yourself just the way you are.

Now tap a positive round to make yourself feel even better. Look at the Tapping Scale and choose a number. Give how you feel a title, such as 'Happy Energy'. Place your hands over your heart in the Heart Healing position, take three deep breaths and state your title. Now tap through all the points while using either the following statements or statements of your own you have created.

TH = Happy Energy.

TE = All this happy energy.

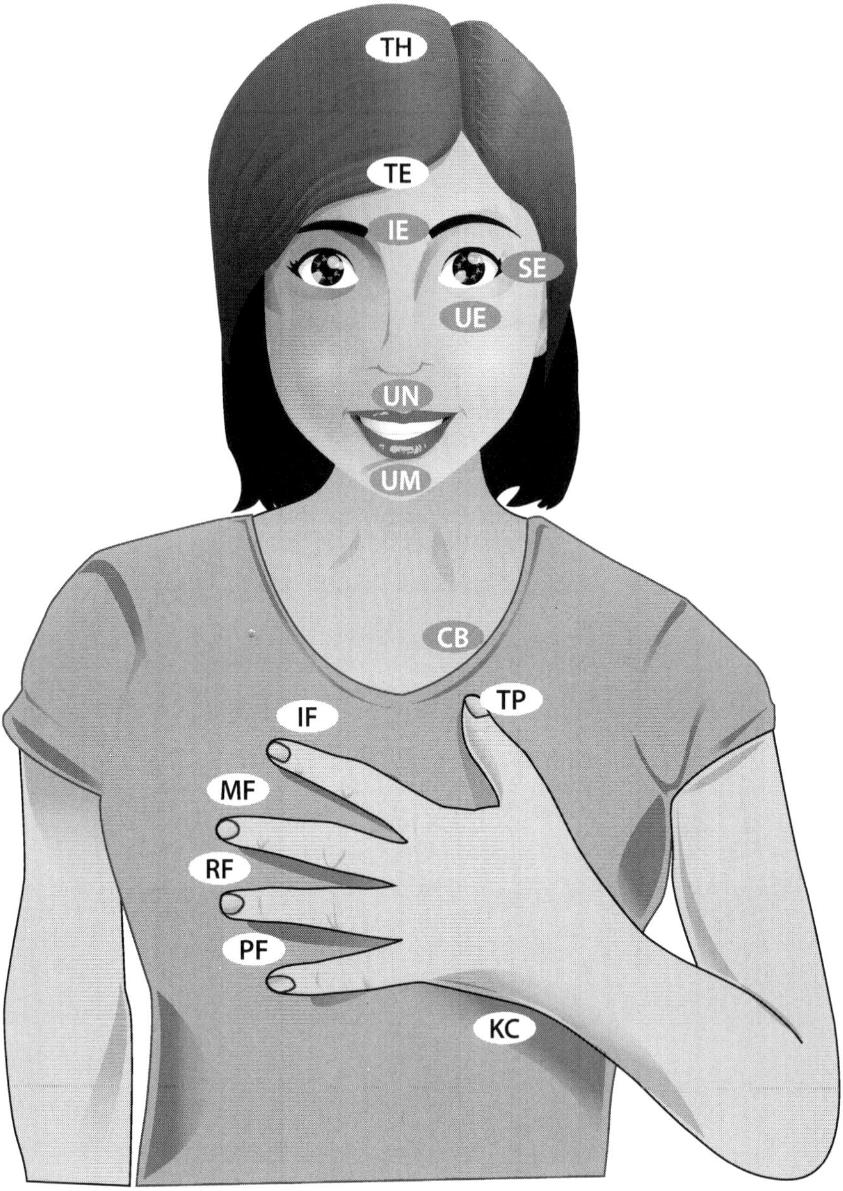
TH
TE
IE
SE
UE
UN
UM
CB
TP
IF
MF
RF
PF
KC

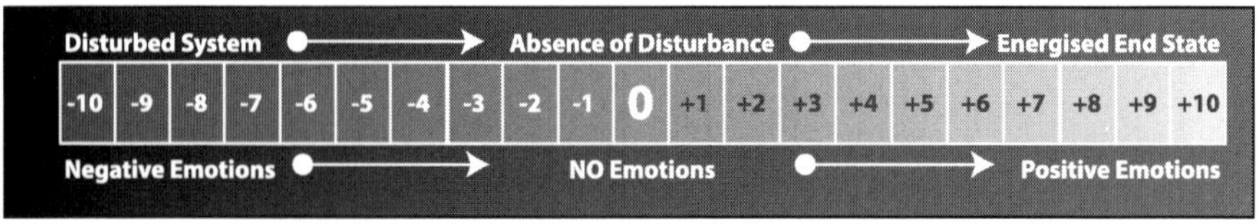
Disturbed System
Absence of Disturbance
Energised End State
-10 -9 -8 -7 -6 -5 -4 -3 -2 -1 0 +1 +2 +3 +4 +5 +6 +7 +8 +9 +10
Negative Emotions
NO Emotions
Positive Emotions

IE = Feeling good.

SE = Feeling positive.

UE = I am okay.

UN = I am feeling good.

UM = I am in control.

CB = I feel calm and confident.

TP = Feeling happy and content.

IF = I am at peace with myself.

MF = I am happy with who I am.

RF = I am enough.

PF = I love and accept myself.

KC = Just the way I am.

Place your hands over your heart in the Heart Healing position and take three deep breaths. Tune into how you are feeling. Are you feeling more positive and more accepting of the way you are? More willing to view yourself in a way that is more accurate instead of the hurtful things people have said to you? More confident? If you have any resistance to saying you like, love or accept yourself, repeat this round a few times.

Tapping to Relieve School Phobias, Anxiety, or Fears About Starting a New School

This is a good tapping script if you are starting at a new school and feeling a little anxious, if you are suffering from a school phobia or just feeling anxious about going to school. Many of us are anxious when trying anything new but learning to manage these anxieties can help us to move forward and feel more confident. Energy EFT is an excellent way to manage your stresses, anxieties and phobias.

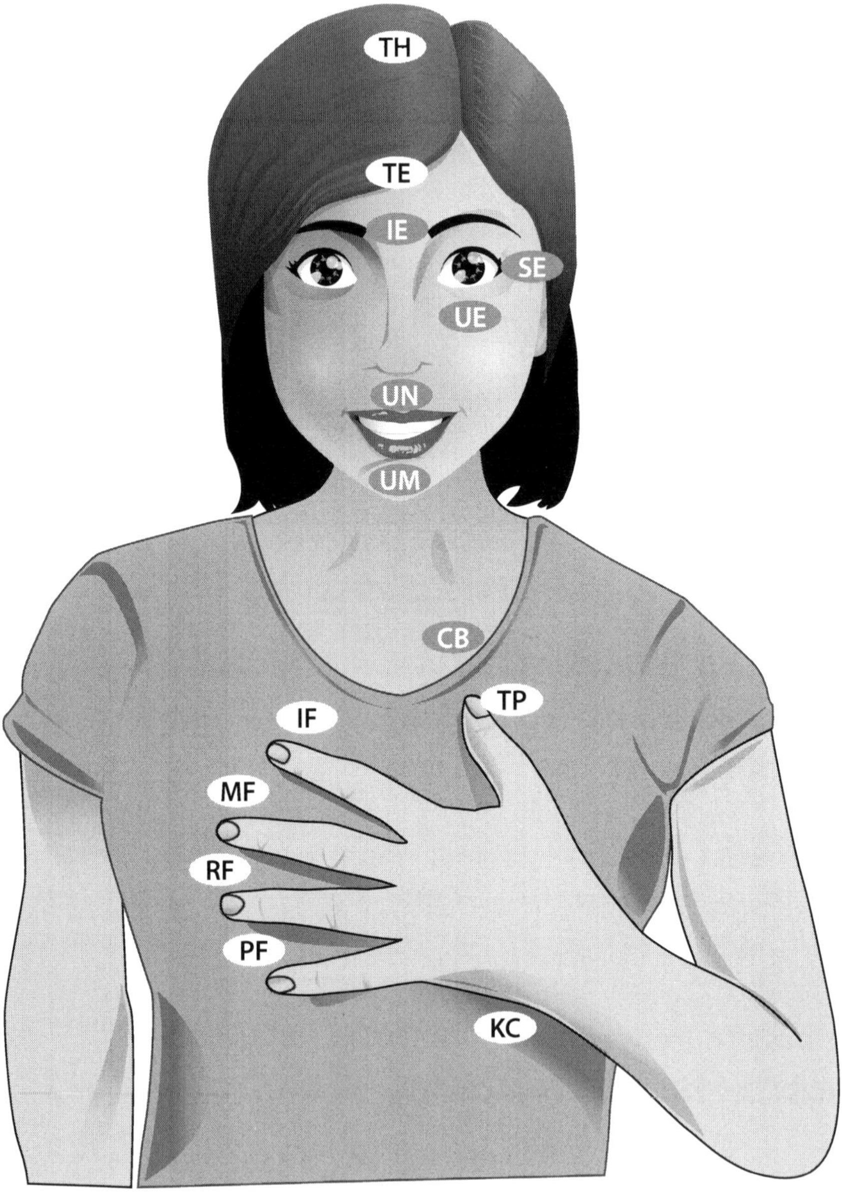
TH
TE
IE
SE
UE
UN
UM
CB
TP
IF
MF
RF
PF
KC

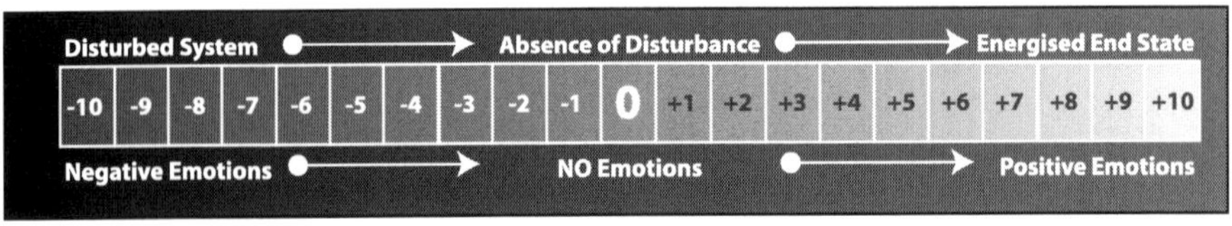
Disturbed System
Absence of Disturbance
Energised End State
-10 -9 -8 -7 -6 -5 -4 -3 -2 -1 0 +1 +2 +3 +4 +5 +6 +7 +8 +9 +10
Negative Emotions
NO Emotions
Positive Emotions

Choose a number on the Tapping Scale that relates to how anxious you are feeling about school. If you are feeling really anxious it is probably somewhere in the minus numbers. Remember the number you have chosen. Give this feeling a title such as 'I Feel So Anxious About Going to School'.

Place your hands over your heart in the Heart Healing position, take three deep breaths and state your title. Now tap through all the points while using either the following statements or statements of your own.

TH = All this anxiety I feel in my body.

TE = Making my stomach feel sick inside.

IE = I feel scared to leave my house.

SE = I hate having to leave my family and familiar things.

UE = I am really worried about going to school.

UN = It is such a big place with lots of people.

UM = I want to stay at home with all my stuff.

CB = All this anxiety I hold in my body.

TP = I choose to let it go.

IF = I choose to feel brave and strong.

MF = Even though I am worried about going to school.

RF = I choose to feel happy and in control.

PF = I choose to relax and feel safe.

KC = All this anxiety, I choose to let it go.

Place your hands over your heart in the Heart Healing position and take three deep breaths. Measure if your anxiety has improved on the Tapping Scale. If you still feel a little anxious, repeat a few more rounds before moving on to the happier tapping sequence.

Choose a number on the Tapping Scale that relates to your revised feelings about school. Remember this number. Give this

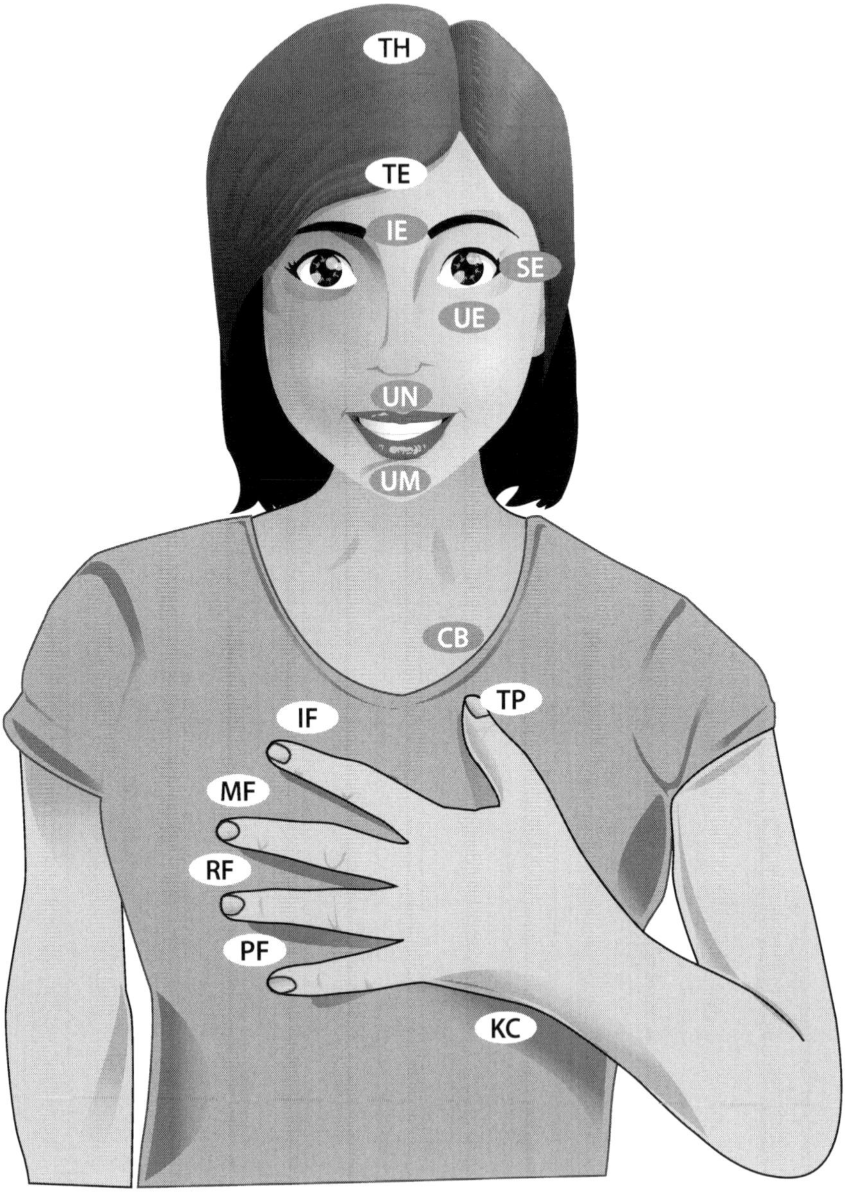
TH
TE
IE
SE
UE
UN
UM
CB
TP
IF
MF
RF
PF
KC

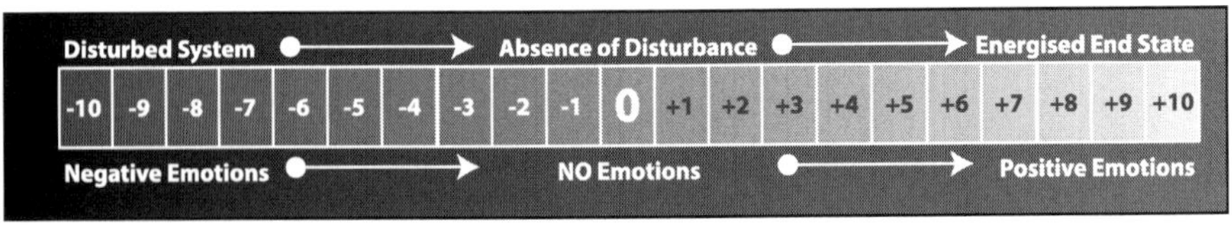
Disturbed System
Absence of Disturbance
Energised End State
-10 -9 -8 -7 -6 -5 -4 -3 -2 -1 0 +1 +2 +3 +4 +5 +6 +7 +8 +9 +10
Negative Emotions
NO Emotions
Positive Emotions

new feeling a title such as 'Feeling Brave'. Place your hands over your heart in the Heart Healing position, take three deep breaths and state your title. Now tap through all the points while using either the following statements or statements of your own.

TH = Maybe I could go to school after all.

TE = It might not be as bad as I think.

IE = I choose to be brave and try new things.

SE = I choose to feel safe and relaxed.

UE = I release this anxiety from my body.

UN = I choose to enjoy doing different things.

UM = I am such a brave kid, brave and strong.

CB = I know I can do this.

TP = Just watch me spread my wings and try new things.

IF = I am brave and happy.

MF = Relaxed and calm.

RF = I choose to feel powerful and brave.

PF = I am awesome.

KC = Just watch me shine like a star.

Place your hands over your heart in the Heart Healing position and take three deep breaths. Check into how you feel on the Tapping Scale and repeat the round a few more times if you need to. By now you are hopefully feeling great and more relaxed about going to school.

Tapping to Relieve Verbal Bullying, Physical Bullying or Cyber Bullying

Bullying can have a serious and devastating effect on a young person's life. It can sometimes be so traumatic it can stay with them for years and, if not addressed, can affect their future life and confidence.

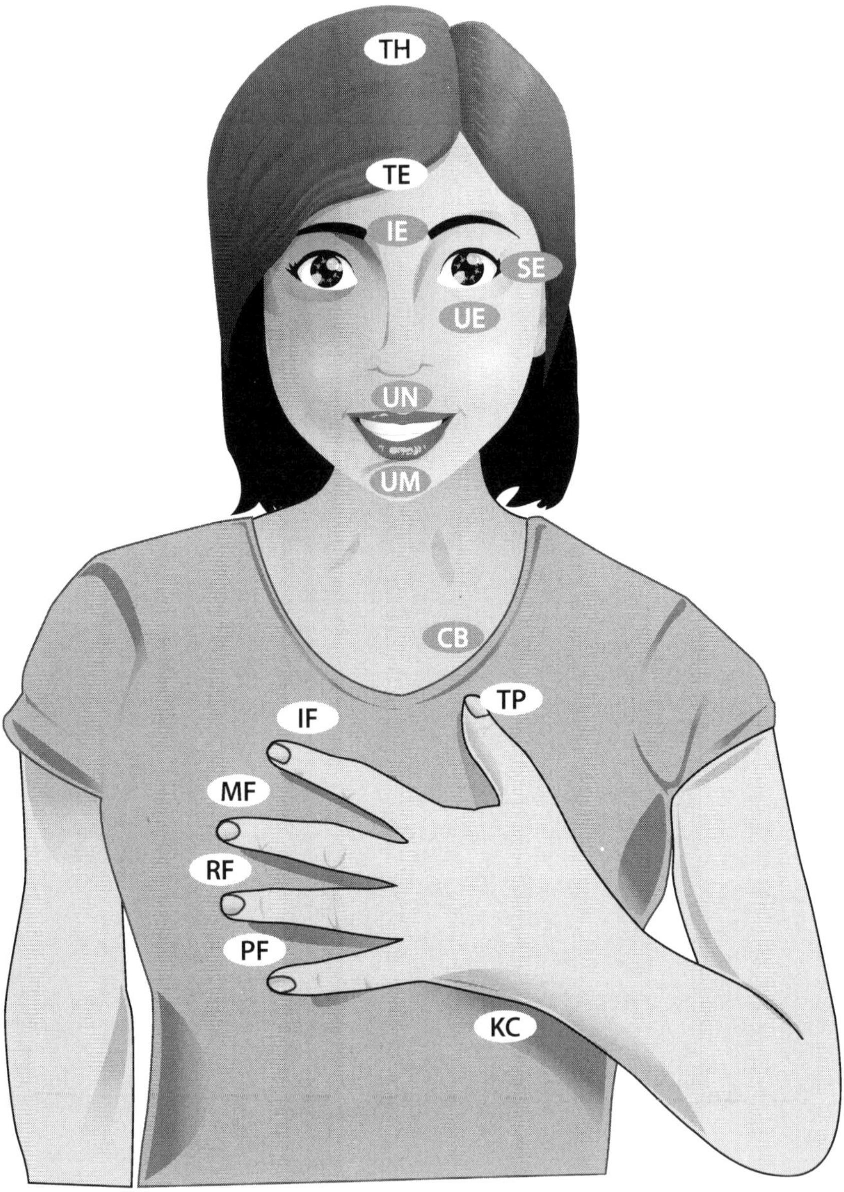
TH
TE
IE
SE
UE
UN
UM
CB
TP
IF
MF
RF
PF
KC

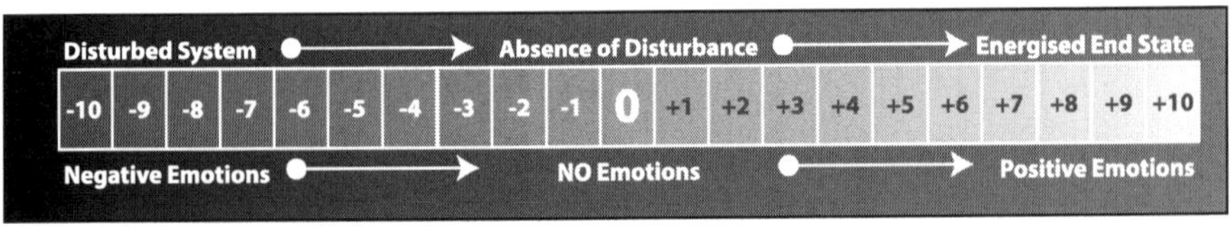
Disturbed System
Absence of Disturbance
Energised End State
-10 -9 -8 -7 -6 -5 -4 -3 -2 -1 0 +1 +2 +3 +4 +5 +6 +7 +8 +9 +10
Negative Emotions
NO Emotions
Positive Emotions

There are many forms of bullying. The three types covered here are Physical, Verbal, and Cyber Bullying. Because these types of bullying are different from each other, they will be split into three sections because each needs to be addressed separately. Energy EFT can really help to lift the stress and anxiety associated with bullying and hopefully help the person being bullied feel a little more able to cope or feel more able to ask for help and support.

Verbal Bullying

Verbal bullying can be very traumatic for the young person on the receiving end. The bully or bullies often exclude, ignore, name call, insult, demean or belittle to bully the person they target. This type of bullying is often difficult to identify because it is usually done when an adult is not around to hear the nasty things being said. This tapping script should help the young person gain back some of their power and raise their self-esteem so they feel they can ask for help.

Choose a number on the Tapping Scale that relates to how you are feeling about being bullied. It will almost definitely be in the minus side of the Tapping Scale. Give this feeling a title such as 'I Am Tired of Being Verbally Bullied'.

Place your hands over your heart in the Heart Healing position, take three deep breaths and state your title. Now tap through all the points while using either the following statements or statements of your own.

TH = I am so fed up of being bullied.

TE = It really makes me feel down.

IE = Why are they so horrible?

SE = I don't deserve all this verbal abuse.

UE = I wish that it would stop.

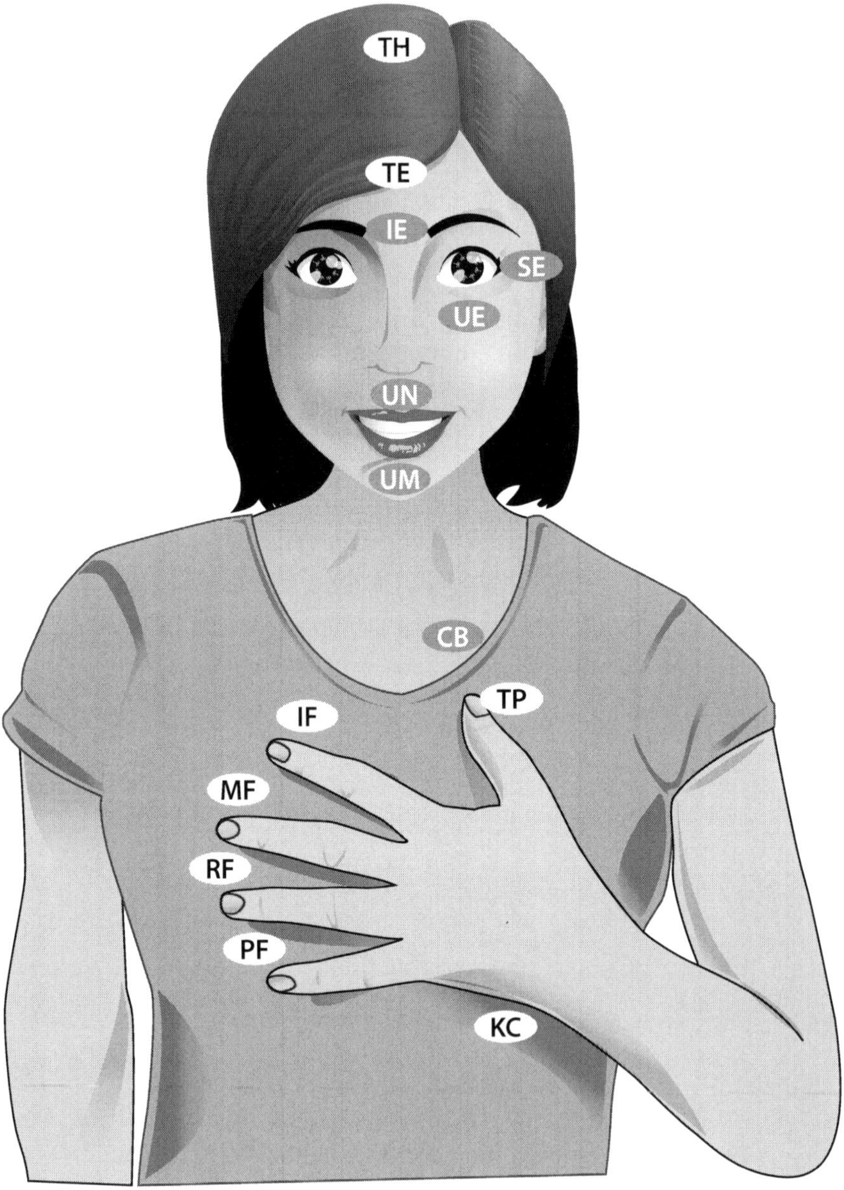
TH
TE
IE
SE
UE
UN
UM
CB
TP
IF
MF
RF
PF
KC

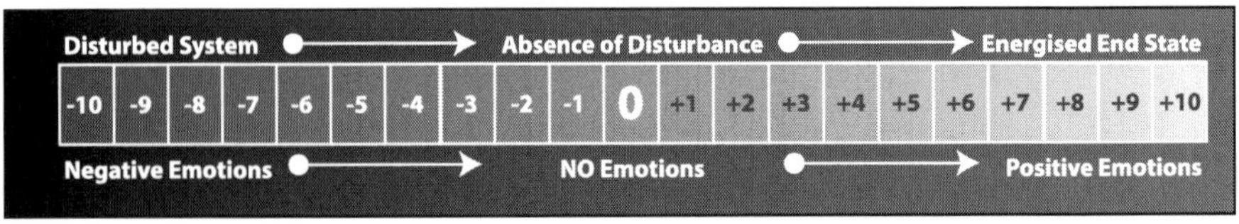
Disturbed System
Absence of Disturbance
Energised End State
-10 -9 -8 -7 -6 -5 -4 -3 -2 -1 0 +1 +2 +3 +4 +5 +6 +7 +8 +9 +10
Negative Emotions
NO Emotions
Positive Emotions

UN = So I can get on with my life in peace.
UM = I hate feeling like this.
CB = But what if I could choose to feel happy?
TP = What if I could ignore all these comments?
IF = After all they are only words.
MF = But it really hurts my feelings.
RF = What if I choose to rise above it?
PF = I could choose to feel empowered.
KC = I choose to release their hurtful words.

Place your hands over your heart in the Heart Healing position, take three deep breaths and let all the negativity go. If you need to, repeat the round a few times until you feel your stress level has diminished.

Choose a number on the Tapping Scale that relates to how you feel now about being bullied. Give this new feeling a title such as 'Feeling More Confident'.

Place your hands over your heart in the Heart Healing position, take three deep breaths and state your title. Now tap through all the points while using either the following statements or statements of your own.

TH = I choose to let all these vile comments go.
TE = I choose to empower my life.
IE = I choose to ignore all these comments and feel relaxed.
SE = I am brave and strong.
UE = I am loved and supported by my family and friends.
UN = The bullies really aren't worth it.
UM = I can fake a smile and walk away.
CB = They will soon get bored if I ignore them.
TP = I am secretly smiling inside.
IF = Because I know I am brave and strong.

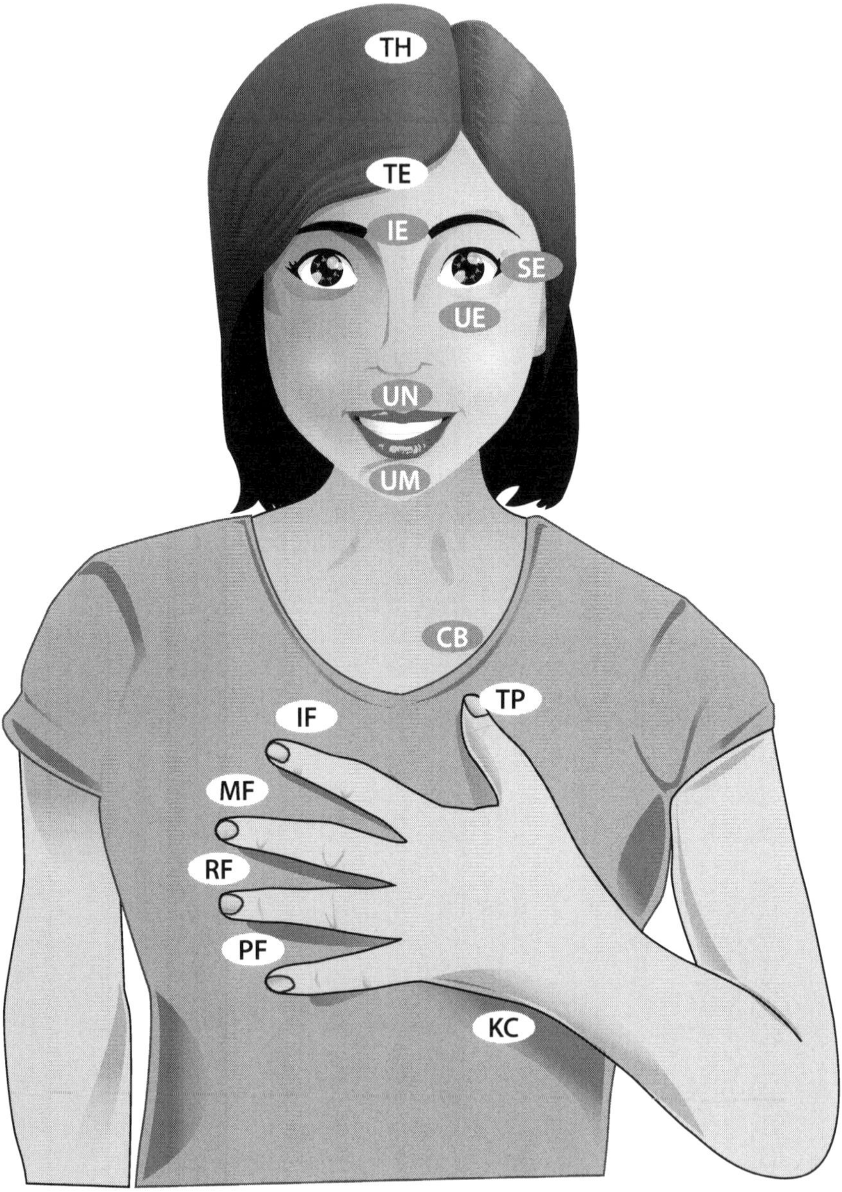
TH
TE
IE
SE
UE
UN
UM
CB
TP
IF
MF
RF
PF
KC

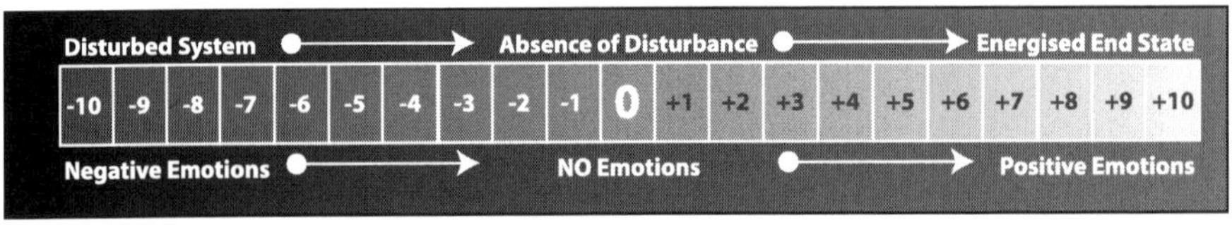
Disturbed System
Absence of Disturbance
Energised End State
-10 -9 -8 -7 -6 -5 -4 -3 -2 -1 0 +1 +2 +3 +4 +5 +6 +7 +8 +9 +10
Negative Emotions
NO Emotions
Positive Emotions

MF = I feel empowered and at ease.

RF = I choose to win this battle by not letting them get to me.

PF = I choose to feel at peace.

KC = I am a brave and strong person.

Place your hands over your heart in the Heart Healing position, take three deep breaths and let all the negativity go. If you are not yet feeling better, repeat this round a few more times. Then ask yourself if the bullying still bothers you. If it does, tap a few more rounds. When you are done tapping, hopefully you will be feeling better and ready to ignore the bully. However, if the bullying continues, please be really brave and ask for help.

Physical Bullying

Physical bullying is the most easy to identify of all the forms of bullying because it often leaves physical evidence and the actions are more visible to other people. Bullies are often bigger, stronger and/or more aggressive than their peers and sometimes they work in groups to gain more power and control over the person they are bullying.

Hopefully the following script will help the person being bullied feel more in control and able to ask for help and support so the bullying can be stopped.

Choose a number on the Tapping Scale that relates to how you are feeling about being bullied. It will almost definitely be on the minus side of the Tapping Scale. Give this feeling a title such as 'I Am Scared of Being Physically Bullied'.

Place your hands over your heart in the Heart Healing position, take three deep breaths and state your title. Now tap through all the points while using either the following statements or statements of your own.

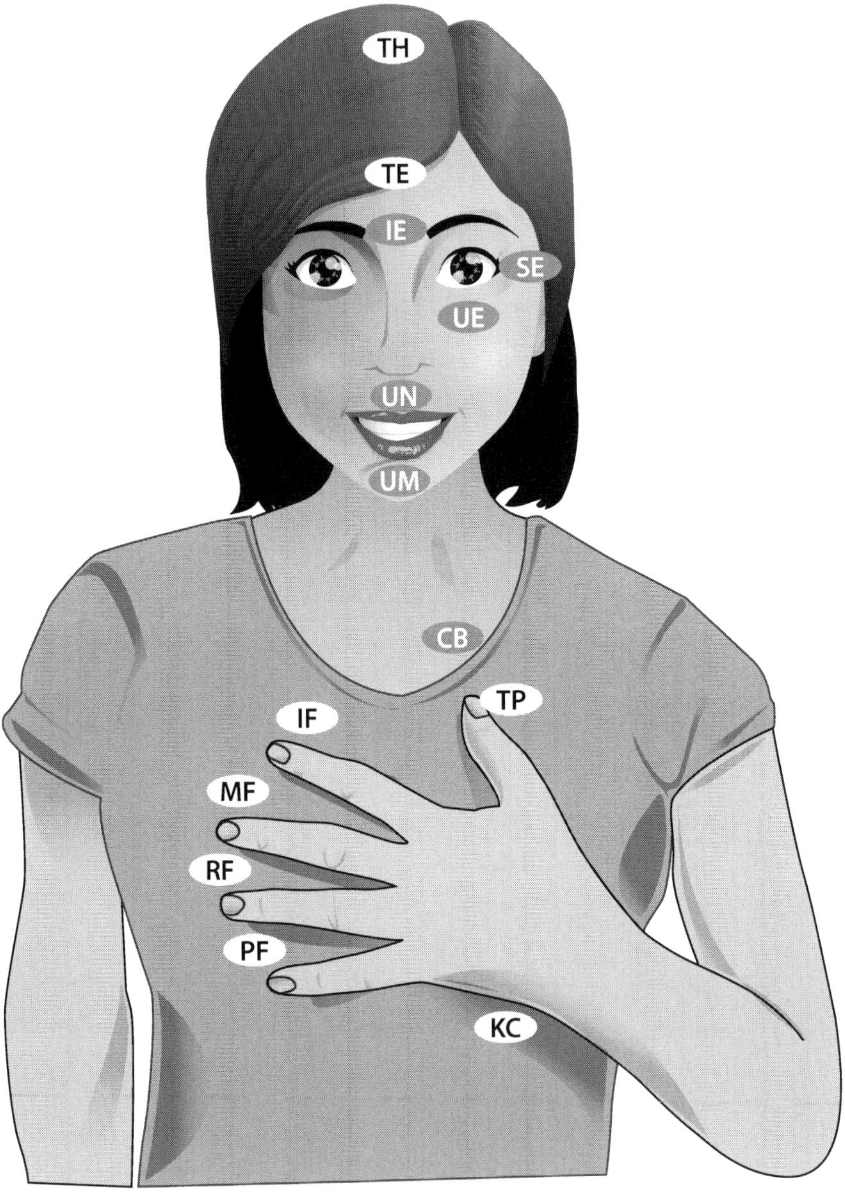
TH
TE
IE
SE
UE
UN
UM
CB
TP
IF
MF
RF
PF
KC

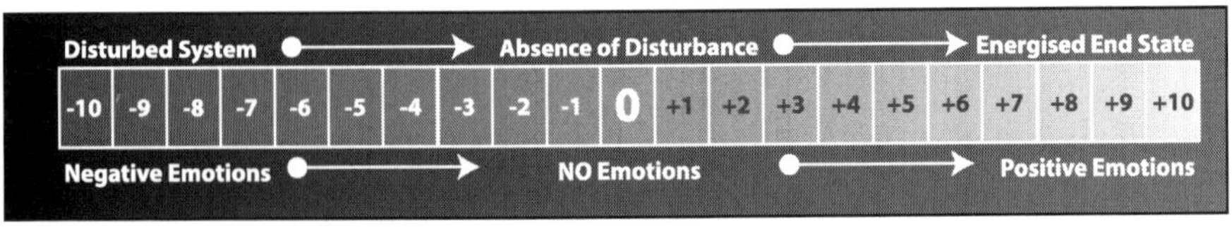
Disturbed System
Absence of Disturbance
Energised End State
-10 -9 -8 -7 -6 -5 -4 -3 -2 -1 0 +1 +2 +3 +4 +5 +6 +7 +8 +9 +10
Negative Emotions
NO Emotions
Positive Emotions

TH = I am so worried about being bullied.

TE = I am too scared to ask for help.

IE = I am worried they might bully me more.

SE = I wish they didn't target me.

UE = All this bullying is affecting my life.

UN = I am constantly looking over my shoulder.

UM = What if there was a way to make them stop?

CB = Could I be brave enough to ask for help?

TP = Maybe I could tell a friend, or a teacher or my Mum?

IF = I shouldn't have to deal with this alone.

MF = I could be really strong and ask for help.

RF = Then maybe it would stop?

PF = I choose to feel really brave about this.

KC = I choose to get some help.

Place your hands over your heart in the Heart Healing position, take three deep breaths and let all the negativity go. If you need to repeat the round a few more times to help improve your stress level.

Once you feel less stressed about being bullied you can tap to make things even better by choosing a positive statement. Choose a number on the Tapping Scale that relates to how you now feel about being bullied. Give this new feeling a title, such as 'Feeling Stronger'.

Place your hands over your heart in the Heart Healing position, take three deep breaths and state your title. Now tap through all the points while using either the following statements or statements of your own.

TH = I am brave and resilient.

TE = I am ready to ask for help.

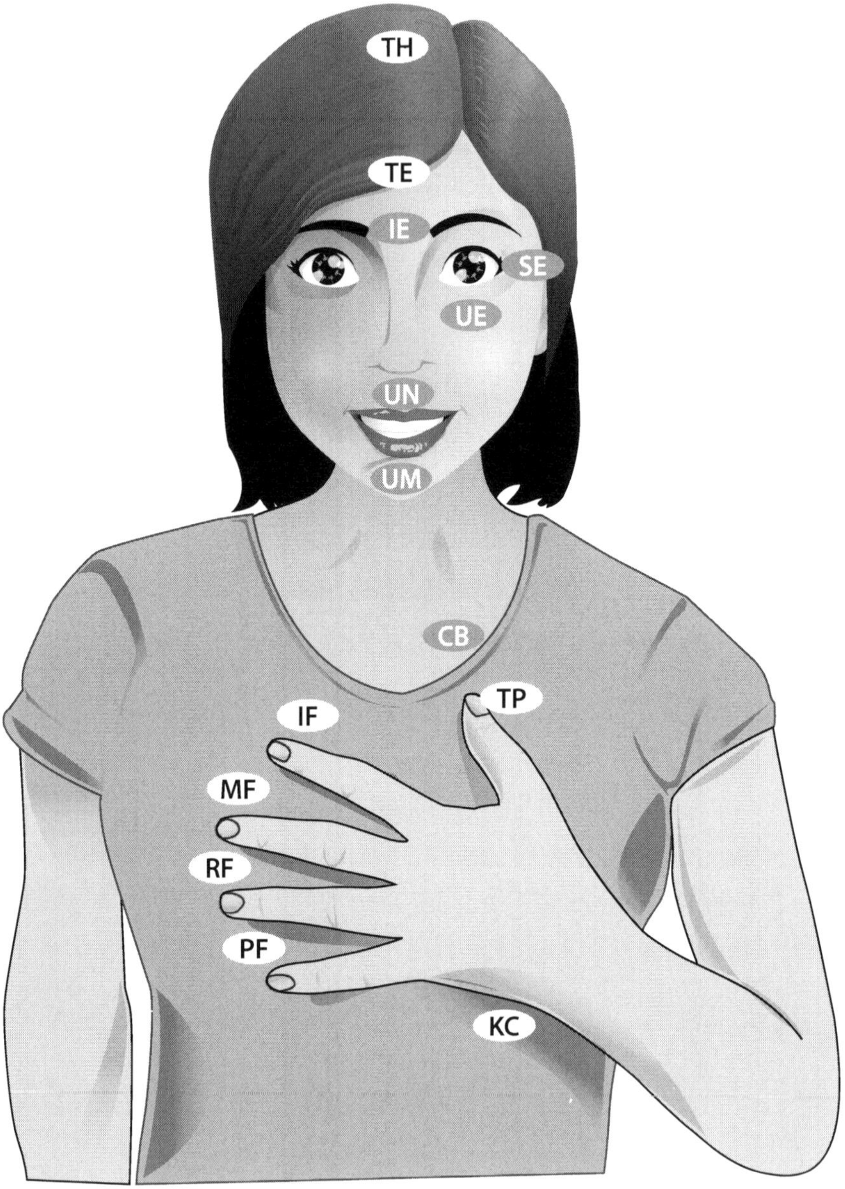
TH
TE
IE
SE
UE
UN
UM
CB
TP
IF
MF
RF
PF
KC

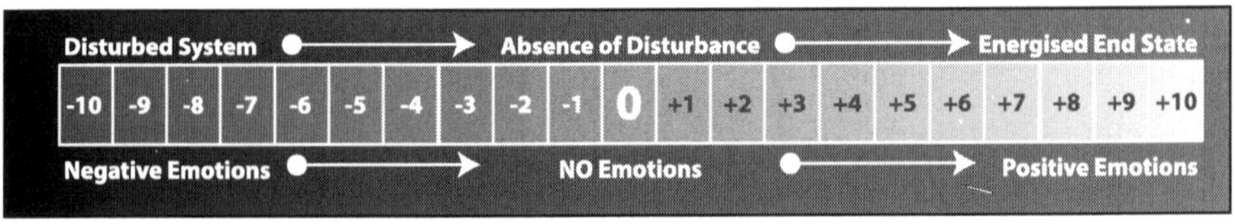
Disturbed System
Absence of Disturbance
Energised End State
-10 -9 -8 -7 -6 -5 -4 -3 -2 -1 0 +1 +2 +3 +4 +5 +6 +7 +8 +9 +10
Negative Emotions
NO Emotions
Positive Emotions

IE = I can be brave and help make this stop.

SE = I can turn things around.

UE = All this bullying has to stop.

UN = I am ready to take control.

UM = This is my life and I choose to be happy.

CB = Maybe I could ask to set up a group in my school?

TP = I can't be the only one being bullied.

IF = Jointly we can make a stand.

MF = I choose to release this fear.

RF = I choose to make things change for the better.

PF = I choose to be happy and brave.

KC = I choose to take control.

Place your hands over your heart in the Heart Healing position, take three deep breaths and let all the negativity go. Repeat the round a few more times if you feel you need to. Check on the Scale to see if your fear has gone down or even disappeared. Ask yourself if the bullying still bothers you. If it does, tap a few more rounds. Hopefully after this you will be feeling brave and ready to reach out to get some help.

Cyber Bullying

Cyber bullying is a totally different type of bullying unique to the digital world. Because it is so anonymous it can be a particularly horrible experience. All bullying is cowardly but this is the most cowardly of all because the person is using a computer screen or phone to hide behind. It leaves the person being bullied scared and paranoid because often they don't know who the bully is.

Choose a number on the Tapping Scale that relates to how you are feeling about being cyber bullied. It will almost definitely

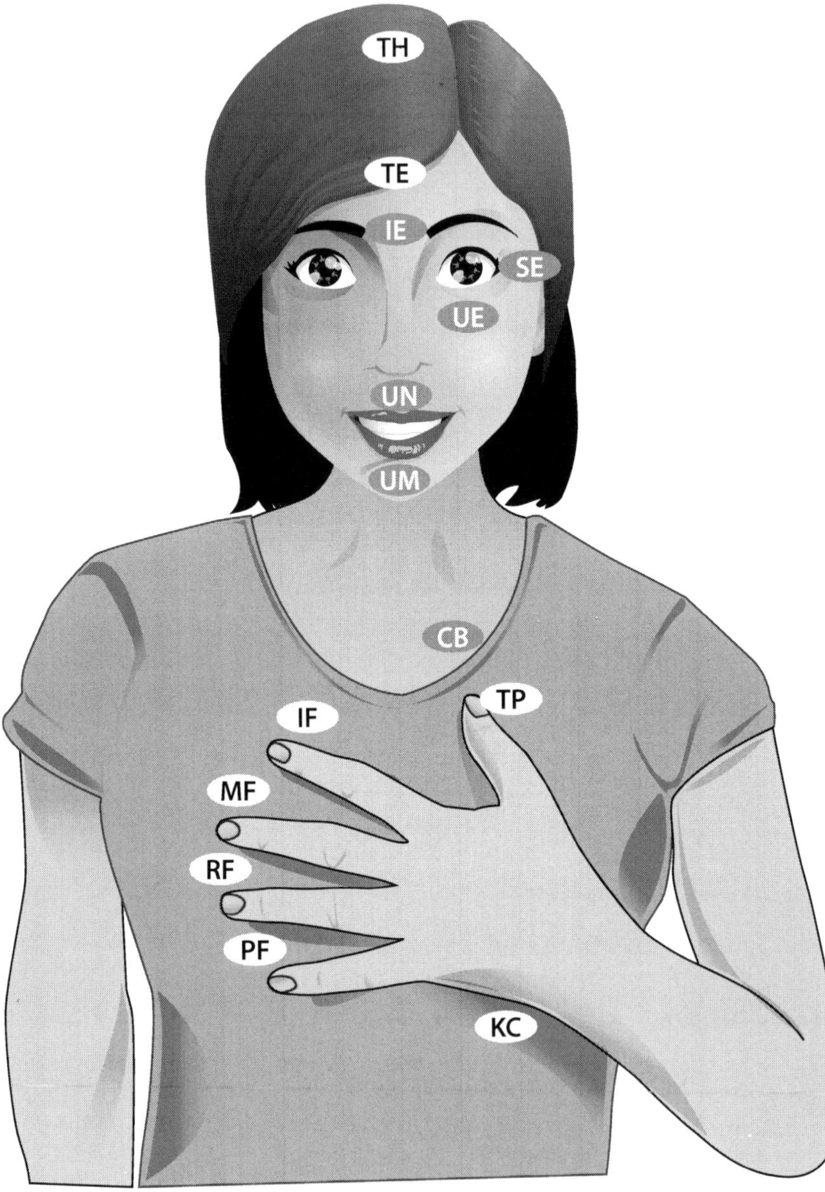
TH
TE
IE
SE
UE
UN
UM
CB
TP
IF
MF
RF
PF
KC

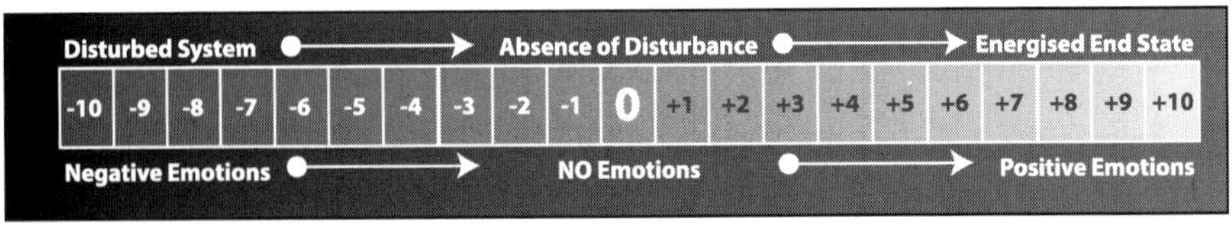
Disturbed System
Absence of Disturbance
Energised End State
-10 -9 -8 -7 -6 -5 -4 -3 -2 -1 0 +1 +2 +3 +4 +5 +6 +7 +8 +9 +10
Negative Emotions
NO Emotions
Positive Emotions

be on the minus side of the Tapping Scale. Give this feeling a title such as 'This Cyber Bullying is Making Me Scared'.

Place your hands over your heart in the Heart Healing position, take three deep breaths and state your title. Now tap through all the points while using either the following statements or statements of your own.

TH = I am scared because I don't know who is bullying me.

TE = They are hiding behind a screen.

IE = I know they are cowards.

SE = But I still don't feel safe.

UE = I wish they would go away.

UN = I want to be left in peace.

UM = I want this bullying to stop.

CB = They target me when I am on my own.

TP = It makes me feel so vulnerable.

IF = But what if I could ask for help?

MF = I could show someone I trust the stuff I am being sent.

RF = Maybe then I could get help.

PF = I could turn this all around.

KC = I could take control of my life.

Place your hands over your heart in the Heart Healing position, take three deep breaths and let all the negativity go. If you need to, repeat the round a few times to see if your stress level has improved on the Tapping Scale.

Once your stress level has improved, tap a positive round to help make you feel even better. Choose a number on the Tapping Scale that relates to how you now feel about being bullied. Give this new feeling a title, such as 'Feeling Brave'.

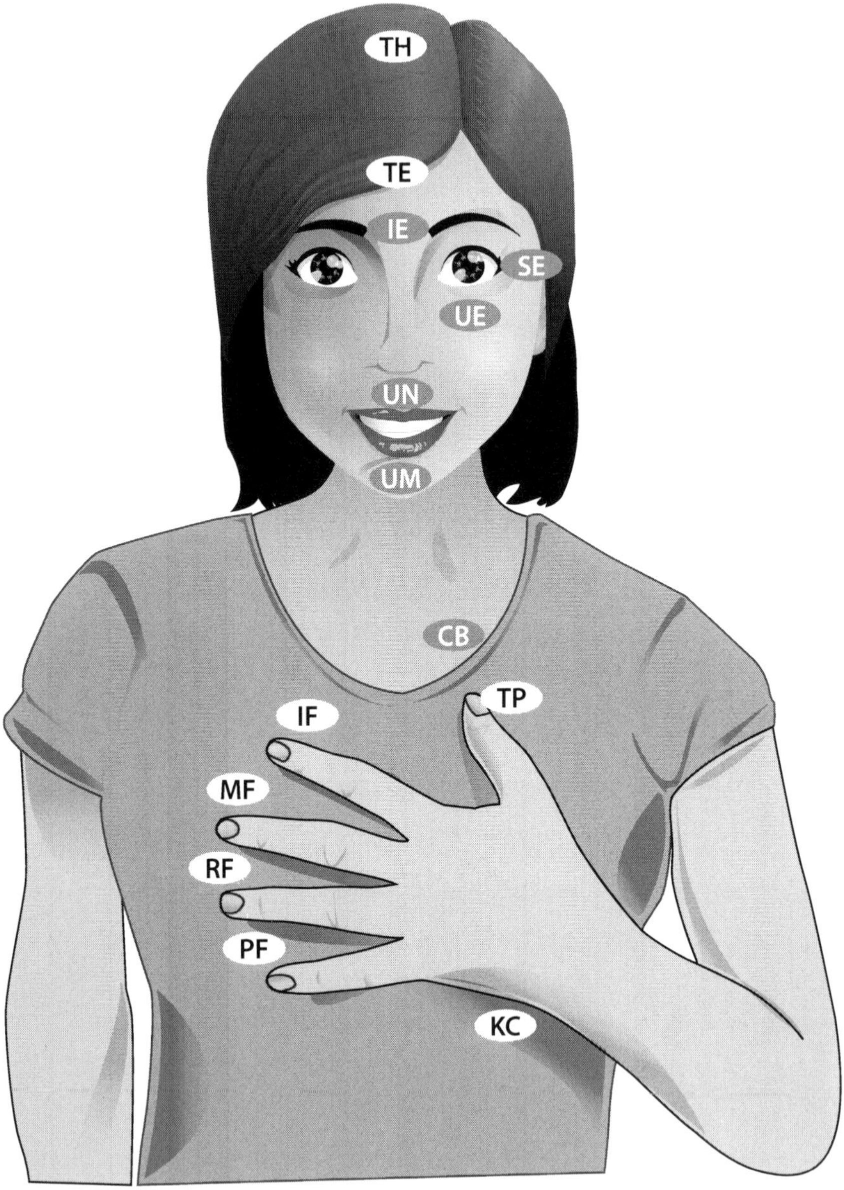
TH
TE
IE
SE
UE
UN
UM
CB
TP
IF
MF
RF
PF
KC

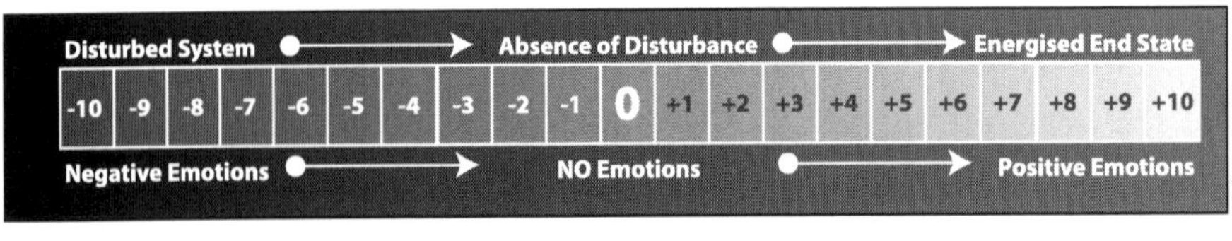
Disturbed System
Absence of Disturbance
Energised End State
-10 -9 -8 -7 -6 -5 -4 -3 -2 -1 0 +1 +2 +3 +4 +5 +6 +7 +8 +9 +10
Negative Emotions
NO Emotions
Positive Emotions

Place your hands over your heart in the Heart Healing position, take three deep breaths and state your title. Now tap through all the points while using either the following statements or statements of your own.

TH = I give myself permission to take control.

TE = I choose to empower my life.

IE = Feeling calm and confident.

SE = I choose to raise my self-esteem.

UE = To be brave and resilient.

UN = To take my power back.

UM = I am worthy of a happy life.

CB = I can be relaxed and happy.

TP = And fill my body with energy.

IF = I can be powerful and in control.

MF = I can get the help I need.

RF = I just have to ask.

PF = It will all be okay.

KC = I choose to take control.

ENERGY EFT FOR SPORTS PERFORMANCE

Many teenagers find sports difficult. At a time when their bodies are changing and hormones are racing, even having to get changed in front of other people to do a sport can cause embarrassment. For other people their worries may be because they feel awkward or feel they will not be as athletic as some of their peers.

Even not getting picked for a team or feeling clumsy when playing a ball game can pose many challenges for a young person at school. It is a time when many would not choose to do sports if

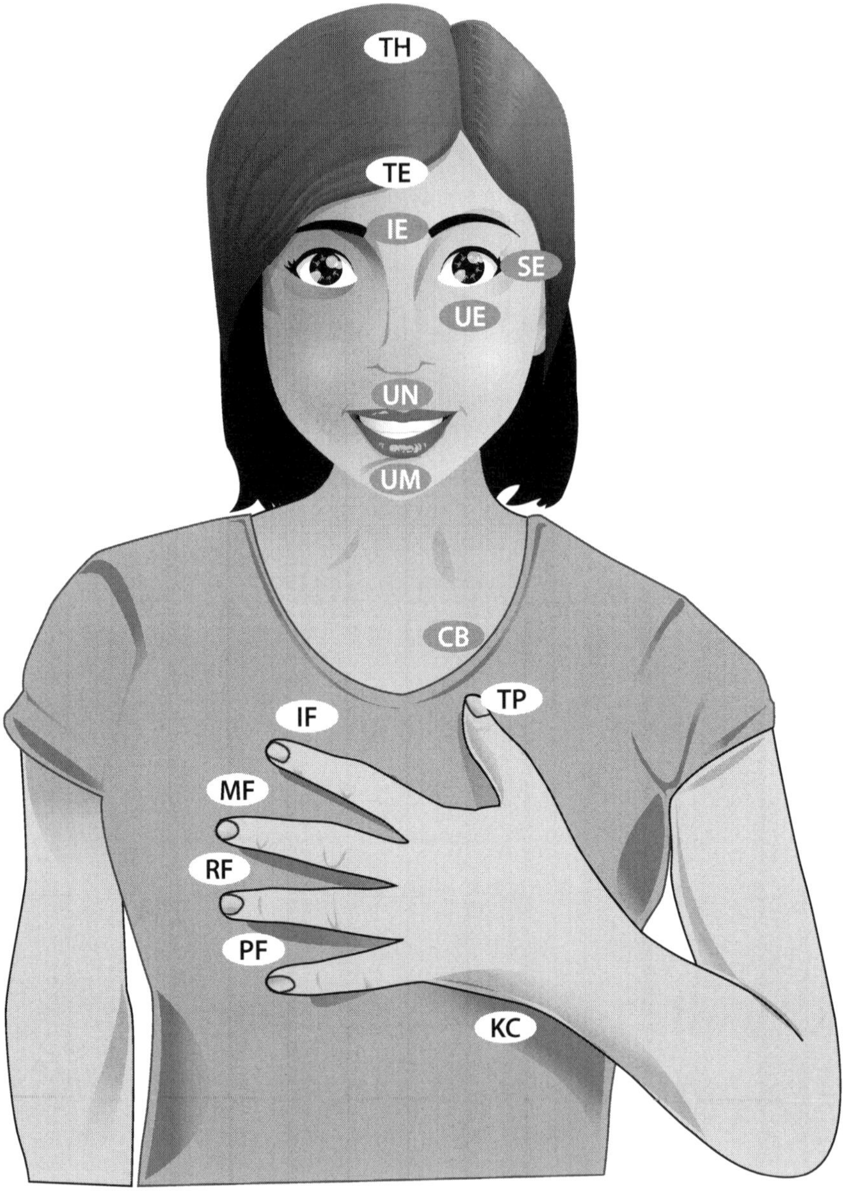
TH
TE
IE
SE
UE
UN
UM
CB
TP
IF
MF
RF
PF
KC

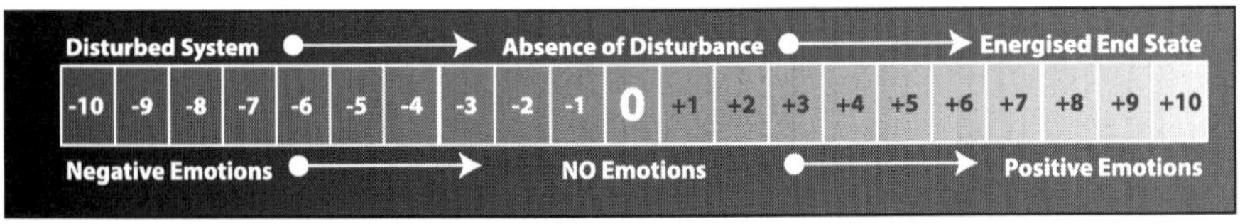
Disturbed System
Absence of Disturbance
Energised End State
-10 -9 -8 -7 -6 -5 -4 -3 -2 -1 0 +1 +2 +3 +4 +5 +6 +7 +8 +9 +10
Negative Emotions
NO Emotions
Positive Emotions

they could but because it is compulsory they know they have no choice. This can cause anxieties before they even get on the pitch.

Being among friends at this time can help to relieve some of the stress but that is not always possible. Many teenagers are worried they will be teased about their abilities, looks or performance and this can actually prevent them from doing well.

Here is a tapping script for general anxieties you might experience when doing sports. There are no specifics about any particular sport or game so the script is geared towards reducing the anxieties and awkward feelings many teenagers get when they are about to participate in any sport.

Choose a number on the Tapping Scale that relates to how you are feeling about participating in a sport. It may be in the minus side of the Tapping Scale if sports are something you dread. Give your feelings a title such as 'I Feel I Am Not Good at Sports'.

Place your hands over your heart in the Heart Healing position, take three deep breaths and state your title. Now tap through all the points while using either the following statements or statements of your own.

TH = I feel like I am useless at sports.

TE = I wish I could do better.

IE = Maybe sports are just not my thing.

SE = But maybe I could improve my technique.

UE = I could try a little harder to concentrate

UN = Maybe I won't be so bad after all.

UM = I am worried people will laugh at me

CB = What if I do something wrong?

TP = This stops me from trying very hard

IF = I feel like I am clumsy and awkward

MF = I don't want to fail or look like a fool

RF = But what's the worst that can happen?

PF = I could learn to laugh at myself and take a few risks

KC = It might not be so bad after all.

Place your hands over your heart in the Heart Healing position and take three deep breaths. Measure if your anxiety about doing a sport has changed for the better.

If the number has improved, tap a positive round to help make you feel even better. Choose a number on the Tapping Scale that relates to how you now feel about being in sports. Give this new feeling a title such as 'I Feel I Can Do Sports'.

Place your hands over your heart in the Heart Healing position, take three deep breaths and state your title. Now tap through all the points while using either the following statements or statements of your own.

TH = Maybe I can learn to be good at sports.

TE = I give myself permission to try.

IE = I choose to up my game.

SE = I choose to try to the best of my ability.

UE = I just need to believe in myself.

UN = I allow myself to feel less anxious.

UM = Who knows what I am capable of?

CB = Just watch me give this a go.

TP = I am sure I can do well.

IF = I can practice until I am good.

MF = Maybe sport can be my thing.

RF = I can relax and learn to enjoy it.

PF = I might even end up loving it.

KC = Just watch me give it a try.

Place your hands over your heart in the Heart Healing position and take three deep breaths. If you feel you need to, repeat the round. Hopefully you will now be on the plus side of the Tapping Scale and feel like taking up the challenge of doing a sport.

CONCLUSION

If you add tapping to your daily life, all sorts of positive changes can occur. You are no longer burdened by old patterns of behaviour and outmoded beliefs; the baggage you carry around like a heavy backpack. You are free to move forward, which can help in so many areas of your life. You are able to attract stronger bonds and friendships, feel better about your abilities and more prepared to cope with the world ahead. Your fight or flight responses are calmed (until needed), your anxieties are greatly reduced and the world seems like a happier, calmer place to live in.

Anytime you experience anything that doesn't help you live a happy life you can literally tap away the negative effects. Energy EFT really is a special tool that you can use at any time. Children, teenagers and adults can benefit from using Energy EFT to help with the daily anxieties and stresses in their lives.

ABOUT THE AUTHOR

I am firstly a mum of three wonderful daughters, two of whom are on the autistic spectrum and the other who is a saint/angel for coping so well with it all. They are my inspiration for writing this book and for sharing the magic that Energy EFT can bring to other teenagers' and families lives.

I am also an artist, an author, a carer, a horse/animal rescuer and rehabilitator, a Reiki Master Practitioner and an Energy EFT Master Practitioner. Over the years I have learned to become a problem solver when the answers for the dilemmas my family was facing just didn't seem to be out there.

The reason I wrote this book was to provide functional help to other Mums, Dads, teenagers, families, care workers/givers and schools where there seems to be little or no help when things go wrong. Their daily lives can be improved by using this profound but simple tapping therapy called Energy EFT.

I have lived and breathed the contents of this book. It is all written from experience and from my searching for answers for myself and my own children when life didn't go quite to plan.

As a family we have faced many problems head on, including Selective Mutism, Sensory Processing Disorder, Asperger's Syndrome, school phobias, severe anxiety, bullying, eating disorders, grief and trauma experiences, extreme stress, low self-esteem, social anxiety, and much more. We have triumphed. My girls are all thriving. Our family life is as stress free and happy as we can make it.

ADDITIONAL READING

BIG Ted's Guide to Tapping
Alex Kent, Illustrated by Jen Smith

Turn Negative Emotions Into Positive Ones with BIG Ted

Join the loveable BIG Ted as he guides you and your child through the near miraculous Emotional Freedom Techniques (EFT). You'll both discover how your emotions are transformed by tapping with your magic finger on points around your face, body and hands.

BIG Ted is suitable for children of all ages and adults will also benefit from joining in with the fun.

Book is available from www.dragonrising.com.

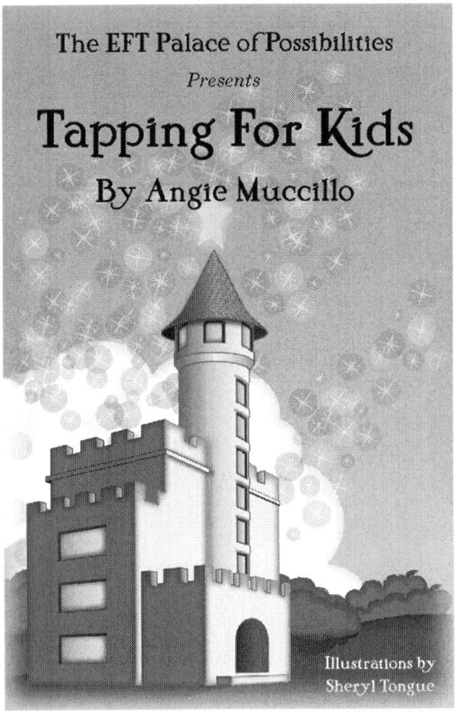

Tapping for Kids—Angie Muccillo

The exciting book aimed at teaching children EFT!

Tapping For Kids is designed to help children overcome traumas and problems of everyday life by using Energy EFT. Through a mix of story, activities and rhymes the book enhances children's learning and shows them how Energy EFT can be used to help them overcome their fears, worries and everyday traumas, while at the same time building up their self-esteem.

The story in the book is set within 'The EFT Palace of Possibilities for Kids', a multilevel healing high rise where its 'Caretaker', known as the TapMeister, runs play shops to help children 'master the art of tapping'—a popular new kids movement taking the world by storm!

The book is filled with illustrations demonstrating how to use the points and numerous exercises to make using Energy EFT fun for kids.

Tapping For Kids is a perfect gift for any children in your life!

Book is available from www.dragonrising.com.

Parenting With Heart and Soul—Kelly Burch

A Parent's Guide to Emotional Freedom with Energy EFT

Parenting is hard. No one tells you that. You suddenly have a child in your care and it's up to you, sink or swim. Ever felt like it should be easier? Yeah, so did Kelly Burch.

In Parenting with Heart & Soul, Kelly combines her expertise as an energy healing practitioner and mother to produce something profound yet also easy to absorb and put into action.

In a straightforward and down-to-earth way, Kelly explains concepts of the energy system and why that matters when it comes to the behaviour of children as well as us parents. She explains what emotions are and how to manage them in children.

Book is available from www.dragonrising.com.

Positive EFT—Silvia Hartmann

Stronger, Faster, Smarter but Most of All, Happier

Positive EFT is the antidote to depression, anxiety, stress, temper tantrums, low energy, misery, impatience, indecision, confusion and feeling helpless, hopeless, powerless and alone. Positive EFT makes introducing EFT an easy, enjoyable, uplifting experience. Perfect for self help and an absolute 'must have!' for the modern practitioner.

Digging around endlessly in the traumas of your past is not the answer to a happy life NOW. By bringing POSITIVE energies into your energy body, you completely transform the way you feel.

Quick and easy-to-use, Positive EFT is an ENORMOUSLY POWERFUL addition to your healing practice. Positive EFT is what the world needs, right now.

Book is available from www.dragonrising.com.

Energy EFT—Silvia Hartmann

Next Generation Tapping & Emotional Freedom Techniques

Silvia Hartmann, chair of The GOE, takes Gary Craig's classic EFT to the next level with this comprehensive book that is an absolute must-buy for anyone interested in energy and its use in turning negative emotions into positive ones. All emotions can be worked with, including Stress, Anxiety, Fear & PTSD. Energy EFT is suitable for both beginners, energy workers in different modalities and also top-level Energy EFT master practitioners & trainers wanting to know more.

Using Energy EFT with energy in mind, you can now experience faster, more focused, more logical Energy EFT self-help treatments and go much further into the realms of empowerment, mental clarity and having all the energy you need to succeed in life.

Book is available from www.dragonrising.com.

Energy EFT Foundation—Silvia Hartmann

The perfect course for you if you would like to learn the Energy EFT tapping system for both self-improvement and helping others.

By learning how to improve energy flow and move further up the SUE Scale, you'll discover how to go from problems to solutions in a broad range of applications. Energy EFT, like its predecessor Classic EFT, teaches you skills about gaining emotional freedom from negative or low energy states, but this updated method is also applicable for creating high-energy states suitable for goal setting, inspiration, creativity and more.

With Energy EFT Foundation, Hartmann has created this highly comprehensive, knowledgeable and practical course, which is packed full of ideas, tips and techniques. This is very much a course for intelligent adults, and you'll have plenty of opportunity putting Energy EFT to work on improving all aspects of your life.

For further details, please visit GOE.ac/foundation

Energy EFT Master Practitioner—Silvia Hartmann

Become Certified as an Energy EFT Master Practitioner.
Available by Live Training or Distance Learning.

The GOE Energy EFT Master Practitioner training takes the developments from the last 15 years of Energy EFT worldwide and brings them together so that the student can experience a clear, logical, direct and powerful way to resolve problems with EFT: Emotional Freedom Techniques.

The successful student will hold the GOE Energy Energy EFT Master Practitioner Certification and can choose to become either a Standard Member or Professional Member of The GOE. Professional Members will be included in the public register to this effect.

Since the time when Energy EFT Emotional Freedom Techniques was first introduced, much has been learned about the cause-and-effect relationships between energy, emotions and how people think, feel and do. Indeed, it was the practice of Energy EFT which led the way to many new discoveries about the basic principles of 'how people work.'

The successful student will gain the GOE Energy EFT Master Practitioner Certification and become a full member of The Association for Meridan & Energy Therapies.

For further details, please visit GOE.ac/eftmp

The Golden Horse

Original Fairy Tales by Silvia Hartmann

Fairy tales especially, with their timeless settings, their powerful imagery and rhythms, their patterns and their unfoldments, shape our lives and thinking more than most will ever know.

The Golden Horse is the perfect antidote for negative 'lessons' taught in traditional fairy tales with powerful stories of true magic, of power, indeed, of our personal, god-given power to change the world and live lives filled with enchantment.

Perfect for sharing with children or the child within, perfect and unusual tools for self help and therapy, these stories can be used to change minds, and hearts, and most of all, re-connect us to the magic we once knew was real when we were still a child.

Book is available from www.dragonrising.com.